BETTER THAN THE TRUTH

"What really happened up in the mountains?" Ann asked, gently touching Lori's arm. "I know it can't be what they're saying."

Dazed, Lori sat down and grabbed the edge of the table. "What exactly *are* they saying, Ann?"

"That stupid Frank O'Conner." Ann bit her lip nervously. "All morning he's been telling everyone that you spent the night with him—alone—in his parents' cabin."

"And you know Fast Frankie—there's slime hanging from every word," Patsy chimed in.

"But I *did* spend the night with him. I had to. We tried to leave the mountains but the troopers told us the roads were closed," Lori explained.

"He didn't mention that part," said Ann. "Maybe you'd better have this out with Frank—before it gets worse."

Lori stood up, her face set and determined. "That's exactly what I'm going to do!"

Merivale Mall

BETTER THAN THE TRUTH

by Jana Ellis

Troll Associates

Library of Congress Cataloging-in-Publication Data

Ellis, Jana.
  Better than the truth / by Jana Ellis.
    p.   cm.—(Merivale mall; #5)
    Summary: Danielle tries to hide the identity of her poor boyfriend
from her rich friends while her cousin Lori finds her relationship
with boyfriend Nick in jeopardy because of rumers.
    ISBN 0-8167-1362-6 (pbk.)
    [1. Cousins—Fiction.]   I. Title.   II. Series: Ellis, Jana.
Merivale mall; #5.
PZ7.E472Bf   1989
[Fic]—dc19   88-15881

A TROLL BOOK, published by Troll Associates,
Mahwah, NJ 07430

BETTER THAN
THE TRUTH

CHAPTER ONE

For what seemed like the zillionth time, sixteen-year-old Lori Randall glanced at the clock over the classroom door. *Countdown continues. Only nine more minutes.* She found it hard to believe, but her long-winded biology teacher, Mr. Harris, was even more boring than usual.

Not that Lori didn't like biology—she did. But Mr. Harris would take half an hour to say something that any normal person would say in five minutes. And his voice sounded like a melancholy bagpipe, one long, monotonous drone. Half the class caught a nap during the period, and the other half tried to wake up the first half.

Lori rubbed at the fatigue in her corn-flower-blue eyes, and picked up her pencil to add a few finishing touches to the outfit she was drawing in her notebook. It was a tailored minidress with a large notched collar and the waist cinched in tight by a wide belt. She could just imagine the new creation in fawn-colored suede with a dark brown alligator belt. She sighed. Fawn-colored suede would set off her long blond hair perfectly. Of course, suede was out of the question on her budget. Saving for college took all her extra money.

"And now, class, I have a real treat," Mr. Harris announced. "An exciting field project."

Treat? He's got to be kidding. Lori moaned to herself. Mr. Harris gave more homework than all her other teachers combined.

"I've broken the class up into two-person teams—" For once, Mr. Harris sounded almost excited. "And I expect each of your teams to *startle* us with unusual specimens. I'm talking about your collecting as many different forms of algae as you can from pond water—freshwater plants, stoneworts, pond scum, you name it! You'll analyze everything and bring it in next week. Remember—the more algae you gather, the more fun we'll have. And, of course, every team will hand in a detailed lab report at that time."

A wave of groans passed over the room. Obviously, no one shared the teacher's enthusiasm for algae or lab reports. Lori made a face; she had no idea what stoneworts were—and she was pretty sure she didn't want to find out!

Lori was straightening up her books, only half listening, when suddenly Mr. Harris's voice jolted her back to reality.

"Lori Randall and Frank O'Conner."

Uh-oh. Lori bit her lip nervously. Working with Frank O'Conner was going to be trouble. He'd been after her since the eighth grade. And now he'd probably think he was going to have his big chance.

But then Lori remembered he didn't like just *her.* He liked all girls. He was very good-looking—tall, broad-shouldered, blond. For a guy with such great looks, it was amazing how often he struck out with girls. But, no, not really that amazing. His whole manner was unbearably obnoxious—he was convinced he was some kind of gift to the female population.

Just a few weeks earlier, Lori had run into him at Merivale Mall and he'd actually asked her out, even though he knew she was going with Nick Hobart. As if she'd do anything to hurt her relationship with the handsomest, sweetest, and most loyal guy in the entire world just so she could go out with a boy whose only dream was to be a Romeo.

Why, oh, why, did she get teamed up with Frank on this biology project!

Lori shot a tentative glance over her shoulder at her "partner." From the back of the room where he always sat, Frank leaned back in his chair, stretched, and winked flirtatiously. Lori rolled her eyes and looked to the front again. Frank was totally impossible. She *had* to get out of this assignment, she just had to.

There was the bell. *Now to talk to Mr. Harris.*

"Remember, everyone—have your specimens ready for next week!" Mr. Harris reminded the class.

In about two seconds the whole class piled out of the room. It was amazing how twenty kids who had been on the edge of deep sleep for almost an hour could wake up and evacuate a room so quickly.

Frank O'Conner, however, did not leave the room. Instead, he walked to the front of the classroom and stood at the head of Lori's aisle waiting for her, a cocky grin on his face. Lori tried to get by him without being impolite —she wanted to catch Mr. Harris before he left to beg him to change her partner.

"Lucky us, huh?" Frank said, tilting his head to one side. Lori wondered how many times Frank had practiced that little tilt of the head in his bathroom mirror. "I've always wanted to be your partner, Lori. I want you to know I'm *real* excited about this . . ." He ran a finger down the sleeve of her blouse.

Lori yanked her arm away, her eyes pure fire. "Listen, Frank," she warned him, "this assignment is strictly business, understand?"

Frank's hand fell back to his side. "Hey," —he shrugged—"I didn't mean anything by it. It's just that I'm looking forward to working with you, that's all."

He seemed genuinely remorseful, and for a moment Lori almost felt sorry she'd come on so strong. "Just so long as you understand," she said.

"I do," Frank assured her. "No funny business. We'll just stick to biology, right?" And he gave her another wink.

"Frank O'Conner, you're impossible!" Lori cried, and brushed past him into the hall. She'd let her guard down for just a moment, and Frank had wasted no time in taking advantage.

There was Mr. Harris, just disappearing around the corner. She had to convince him to change her partner. A week of dealing with Frank O'Conner would be a fate worse than death!

"Mr. Harris!" The teacher stopped when he heard his name called. Lori moved quickly to meet him, her blond hair flying out behind her.

"Mr. Harris, I need to ask you a favor,"

she began. "See, my partner for the assignment—Frank O'Conner—I, um . . ."

"Yes?" The teacher was looking at her attentively.

Why couldn't she just come out and ask him? Because it sounded so petty, asking to change her lab partner. She couldn't very well tell Mr. Harris *why* she wanted to switch. "Um, do you think I could be paired with somebody else?" she asked lamely.

"Lori"—the teacher smiled—"if I let you pick your own partner, I'd have to let everyone in the class do the same. We can't have that, can we? No. I know Frank isn't the most diligent student, but I'm sure if you insist on it, he'll carry his own weight. Besides—"

Mr. Harris was doing his usual number, running on and on, when all he really had to say was no. Crestfallen, Lori heaved a giant sigh. "Never mind, Mr. Harris," she said, interrupting him. She was already late for English, and she didn't want to be later. Also, she didn't want to annoy Mr. Harris. She'd just have to deal with Frank herself.

Frank cornered Lori later in study hall. "Listen, Lori," he whispered, leaning close to her. "I've got this great idea for our project."

"Oh?" Lori looked him right in the eye, trying to see through to that devious brain of his. Was it possible Frank was really going to keep his slimy intentions to himself and keep his mind on their slimy algae? "Well, what is it?"

"You're going to love this, Lori—we'll get an A for sure. Listen. Harris wants us to gather *unusual* specimens, right? Well, everyone's going to be scooping stuff up from the same places—the brook behind the mall, Finley's Marsh—but I know a place where we can get stuff nobody else'll have!"

Hmmm, thought Lori, searching Frank's penetrating green eyes. *He really seems sincere about this.* "Okay, Frank, where do we go to get these unique treasures?"

"Aha!" crowed Frank in a too loud whisper, drawing angry stares from kids who were trying to concentrate. "Get this. We take a ride way up into the mountains, to around the Oakdale area. There're lots of great ponds and lakes up there! It's an A plus for sure, Lori."

"Oakdale, huh?" Lori had to hand it to Frank—going out of town to get specimens. Maybe she had misjudged him. . . . "That sounds good. How'd you think of a place like Oakdale?"

"Oh, I've been up there lots—my folks have a little cabin there—"

"Wait a minute, Frank!" Lori interrupted, but then stopped herself. She felt slightly uncomfortable, but decided not to be negative. Just because his folks had a cabin in the mountains didn't mean they'd be anywhere near it.

"Gee, Lori, I didn't mean anything, I swear! I only thought we could ace the assignment this way, that's all." He shrugged, and shook his head in disappointment.

Lori looked at him. Maybe she'd been too harsh. After all, it *was* a good idea, and she *did* want to get an A in bio. . . . She smiled at him and nodded her head.

"Great, Lori!" he said happily, drawing another round of angry stares. "I'll call you tonight to set everything up." Just then the bell rang and he packed up his books and strode out of the room, a noticeable bounce in his step.

Lori looked after him, feeling a knot form in the pit of her stomach. Frank always had something up his sleeve—could he be planning a sneak attack?

CHAPTER TWO

"You're going where with him?!" Ann Larson and Patsy Donovan chorused, staring at Lori across the table in disbelief.

"Come on, you guys, it's only a biology assignment," she protested weakly to her two best friends.

Patsy rolled her hazel eyes. "All I can say is good luck, Lori. You're going to need it." Patsy decided to say nothing more, so she took a bite of her salad. "Mmmm—Cornucopia's the greatest, isn't it?" she cooed, changing the subject purposely. "I never knew salad could taste so good."

Lori shot Ann an amused glance. Ann's wide gray eyes twinkled with merriment. The girls had always preferred eating healthfully, which was probably why they never had

weight problems. Ann had a spectacular figure and kept it that way because she worked
out every day. She was an aerobics instructor
at the Body Shoppe. As for Lori—well, she
was just one of those people whose metabo-
lism makes everybody jealous. She could eat
whatever she wanted and never gain an
ounce.

Their friend Patsy, however, was a different story. Lori and Ann could both remember the not-so-long-ago days when Patsy
was looked on as a candidate for Weight
Watchers. Her job at the Cookie Connection
had helped to balloon her weight up. And
when she wasn't eating her own wares, she
was visiting Lori, who worked at Tio's Tacos,
and munching cheese enchiladas.

That had all changed, of course. Now
Patsy Donovan was a model of dietary disci-
pline. She'd lost so much weight that she'd
been crowned Miss Merivale Mall, beating
out every gorgeous girl in town, including
Lori's rich cousin, Danielle Sharp. So now,
when the three friends met for their supper
break, it was always salad at Cornucopia. It
got a little boring for Lori and Ann, but for
Patsy's sake they were willing to munch buck-
ets of greens. After all, the three of them
were best friends.

"So, when are you and Frank O'Conner
going off to the mountains together?" asked

Ann with an ironic grin as she straightened her french braid and tucked a stray lock of shiny brown hair behind her ear.

"I don't know yet. This weekend I guess. Frank's supposed to call tonight with a plan. I guess I'll have to take time off from Tio's—"

"Or from Nick," Patsy threw in. "Speaking of which, does he know about this little plan of yours?"

"Hey, Pats, it's not my plan, you know! The whole thing was Frank's idea. I just thought it was a good one—we're sure to get an A."

"Lori, what's an A if it means the end of your relationship with Nick?" asked Ann, her face suddenly serious.

"Oh, come on, you guys, Nick will understand. He trusts me completely, and why shouldn't he?"

"Have you told him yet?" Patsy asked, pressing her.

"Well, no. I called, but I missed him. Besides, he's going to his dad's warehouse to take inventory this weekend, so we couldn't go out anyway. I'm sure he won't mind—"

"Okay, Lori," said Ann dubiously. "As long as you're sure—"

"Better let him know in advance though," Patsy warned. "Even the most understanding guy in the world won't understand *some* things, especially if they come after the fact.

Frank O'Conner isn't called Mr. Sleaze for nothing, you know."

Lori rolled her eyes in mock frustration. "Quit it, you guys, will you?" She laughed. "It's not like we're staying overnight—we're going for the day, at most!"

"Whatever you say, Lori," said Ann. "But it's not us you have to convince—it's Nick."

After they finished eating, Patsy popped her giant chocolate-chip-cookie hat on her head and ran off to work. "Bye," yelled Lori and Ann.

Ann ambled down the third-level promenade to the Body Shoppe, while Lori took the escalator to the first floor. She made her way over to Hobart Electronics, which was just across from Tio's. "Is Nick around?" she asked a salesman.

"Nope. He just left for the warehouse with his dad. Want me to give him a message?"

Lori thought for a moment. How did she keep missing him? "Well, no, I guess not." She'd wait for Frank's call, then fill Nick in on the plans by telephone. But now it was time for work.

"Lori!"

Turning toward the familiar voice, Lori watched her cousin Danielle Sharp run down the promenade toward her, that fabulous red hair of hers spun out behind her in soft flowing waves.

"Hi, Dani! Haven't seen you in a while," said Lori, giving her cousin a quick kiss on the cheek.

It was true. The cousins didn't see much of each other these days. Once, they'd been really close, more like sisters than cousins. But ever since Danielle's father, Lori's uncle Mike, had made his money and sent Danielle to a private school, the two girls had drifted further and further apart. Danielle hung out with the wealthy Atwood Academy set now, girls like Teresa Woods and Heather Barron, and she never included Lori in anything she did with them. In fact, Lori knew that Danielle was actually embarrassed to have a cousin who went to public school and who had to work at Merivale Mall for spending money.

"How've you been, Lor?" asked Danielle, her cheeks flushed from running.

"Oh, okay, I guess—" said Lori, wondering why Danielle dropped by. Lori knew Danielle must want something from her.

"Come on, you can't fool me—you look like you just got bad news. What's up?"

"Oh, it's nothing. I've got to do a biology project with Frank O'Conner, that's all. We're going up to the mountains together—"

"Did you say that's all?" Danielle's emerald eyes lit up, and she ran her hand up and down the sleeve of her new fox jacket. "You and Frank, together, up in the mountains?

Does this mean you and Nick are no longer an item?"

Ah! thought Lori. *Dani must have heard about my little trip and that's why she's here.* Lori knew exactly what Danielle was thinking. If Lori really were breaking up with Nick, Danielle might be after him in no time!

"It doesn't mean that at all! Nick and I are doing just fine, Dani," Lori assured her cousin. Was she imagining it, or did Danielle look disappointed?

"That's great, glad to hear it," said Danielle halfheartedly. "Well, let me know if things change, okay? I'm always interested in your love life, Lor."

Sure you are, thought Lori. *As long as it involves Nick Hobart.*

"Well, I've got to run," announced Danielle. "Great to see you, Lor. We'll have to get together."

"When?" Lori asked innocently, knowing that Danielle didn't *really* mean they'd get together.

"Oh. Gosh. Soon, very, very soon. I'll call—okay?" And Danielle ran off as breathlessly as she had arrived.

As Lori turned to walk into Tio's Tacos, she was smiling.

Checking her face in her compact mirror and then applying a fresh coat of Brazen lipstick, Danielle slipped into Video Arcade. She checked first to make sure that Teresa, Heather, or any of her other friends were nowhere in sight. The last thing Danielle wanted right then was to be spotted by her superwealthy, supersnobby friends.

There he was! Standing at the Power Drive game, racking up points, intensity written all over his rugged, handsome face, was Don James. He had always attracted Danielle, but, of course, any relationship between them would be absolutely impossible.

After all, she was Danielle Sharp, the queen of Atwood Academy's most popular crowd, the very essence of class—

And he was Don James, a boy who attended public school and ran with the leather-jacket set. He lived in a rundown farmhouse on the wrong side of town with a few other guys, and aspired to be only an auto mechanic. No girl in her right mind would be caught dead with him.

But, oh, he was gorgeous, so—so—oooh, Danielle just couldn't stay away from him. Whether it was his gypsy-dark eyes, glossy jet-black hair and sensational body, or his sense of humor and gentleness, Danielle couldn't have said. All she knew was that he really got to her in a big way, and it drove her up a wall not to go out with him—if she wanted to hold on to her position and reputation at Atwood.

Still, she could flirt with him—if they bumped into each other.

"Oh, hi, Don," she said, sidling up behind him, and trying to sound as if she'd run into him by accident.

Don James looked up from his game, his dangerous grin slowly lighting up his face. "Hey, Red!" he drawled. "Changed your mind about being seen with me?"

"Of course not!" said Danielle, a little too forcefully. "I—"

"What?" he demanded. "You what? Did you leave your fancy friends waiting on the top level of this mall and come all the way down here—looking like a million bucks—just to tell me you won't be seen with me?"

"Well, I—" Darn him! He always could see right through her. Maybe that was something else she liked so much about him.

"Come on, Red," he said, leaning back against his video game and crossing his arms over his chest. "I know what your friends say about me, but you and I both know it's not true—I'm a nice guy, really I am."

"I know you are, Don," she said softly. It was true. Don James's reputation was mostly legend and very little fact. But still, if her friends ever got wind she was hanging around with him, it would be a social disaster for her.

"Come on—take a chance. Let's go out.

What do you say? We had pizza together once and had a terrific time—"

"I can't, Don, sorry," she interrupted.

"It's your friends, isn't it?" he said. "You'd go out with me if it weren't for them. I know you would."

"It has absolutely *nothing* to do with them, honestly!" she lied. Telling the truth would make her look like a slave to her status.

Danielle let her gaze fall to the floor. She hated to think it, but maybe her friends' opinions were more important to her than her own.

"Come on, I dare you," he whispered, a challenge in his voice. "If you don't have a good time, you never even have to look at me again."

She did have fun with him, and he always made her laugh. And more than anything she wanted to go, but—

"Well—all right," she agreed, looking over her shoulder nervously to make sure nobody important was around.

"You won't regret it!" Don touched her on the arm, sending a shiver up and down her spine. "I'll pick you up Saturday night at seven."

"Let's take my car, okay?" Danielle interjected. The last thing she needed was to be seen in Don's beat-up T-Bird. Her sleek white BMW was a much better way to travel.

"Whatever you say." He shrugged. "And don't worry, Red—I'll be a perfect gentleman."

Danielle looked up into his smoldering dark eyes and saw the hint of laughter in them. Then she gave him a dazzling smile. *Not too perfect*, she hoped.

CHAPTER THREE

As far as Lori was concerned, Saturday morning had arrived much too quickly. She felt like crawling out of her bed and straight under a rock. How was she ever going to make it through an entire day with Frank O'Conner?

She slipped out of bed and into the shower. Back in her room she heard her eight-year-old brother, Mark, yell from down the hall. "Some guy is here to pick you up!"

Lori glanced at her clock radio. It was eight-forty. She should have been ready at eight. "Tell him I'm not ready yet, Mark. I'll be there as soon as I get dressed," she called back.

If only she'd been able to reach Nick on Thursday night after work, or Friday, but she had missed him every single time she called. When she phoned his house, he was working at the store, when she called the store, he was out at the warehouse and no one could locate him there.

It was impossible. Simply leaving a message wouldn't have done in this case. What could she say? "Tell him I went up to the mountains with Frank O'Conner?" Under the circumstances, Lori thought it was important to tell him herself what was happening.

Lori picked up her hot pink Trimline phone and dialed Nick's number. *Please don't have gone to work already.* She let it ring a dozen times. But finally realizing Nick wasn't there, she put down the receiver. Talking to Nick would just have to wait. Lori promised herself she'd reach him one way or another the second she got back from the trip, and apologize her head off for not being able to reach him sooner.

Reaching for a pair of jeans and a fleecy sweat shirt, Lori checked herself out in the full-length mirror on the back of her closet door. *Ugh.* No guy could possibly be attracted to her in that outfit—not even Frank O'Conner. But the clothes were perfect for wading in marshes and slogging through the mud.

"Lori?" Her mother's voice sounded tentative.

"Come in, Mom!" Lori called, pulling a

brush through her long blond hair and reaching for a barrette.

"I brought you an English muffin. I didn't want you skipping breakfast," said her mother, leaving a plate on Lori's bureau.

"Well, you are a nurse. Whatever you say," Lori replied with a smile, picking up a piece of muffin and biting into it. "Let's see, I'd better take an extra sweater—"

"Oh, by the way, Nick called." Her mother sounded so matter-of-fact when she said it.

"Nick called? When?" Lori tried to keep the desperation out of her voice, but she couldn't do it.

Mrs. Randall's gray-blue eyes widened. "Just a little while ago."

"Oh, Mom!" moaned Lori. "Why didn't you get me!"

"Well, you were in the shower, honey."

"Oh, never mind, it's okay," said Lori, trying not to sound too grumpy as she pulled on her old hiking boots. The day wasn't exactly getting off to a terrific start.

"Hey, Lori!" Mark shrieked. "Hurry up! Frank's still waiting."

"Tell him I'll be right there, okay?" said Lori, picking up a notebook and pen. "Well, I'd better get going."

Lori's mother looked at her daughter with concern. "Are you sure this is a good idea, honey? The weatherman predicted snow up in the mountains for later today. Maybe you should go another day. . . ."

Lori sighed. If only she *could* put it off until Sunday— She'd have time to tell Nick about the trip, and she wouldn't have to face Frank right now. But it was too late. She'd already asked Ernie Goldbloom, her boss at Tio's, for the day off, and he'd arranged for a replacement. Going the next day would mean another day's pay lost.

Besides, maybe it was just as well. If the weather got nasty, they'd just have to come back early, a prospect that was fine with Lori.

"Can't do it any other day, Mom. The project's due next week. But we won't stay long. Collecting algae with Frank O'Conner isn't my idea of fun. Oh, and, Mom, if Nick calls again, tell him I'll call as soon as I get back, okay? And really, don't worry. I'll make sure we're back before dark."

"Well, all right," her mother replied. "Have a good time, Lori."

"I'll try. Bye!" Lori blew her mother a kiss and hurried into the living room. There was Frank, with Mark as a captive audience. "So the pitcher stepped up to the mound and *wham*! Oh! Hi, Lori! Well, Mark, to be continued," he said, pulling Mark's baseball cap over his eyes playfully. "We've got to go."

"Hi, Frank," said Lori, trying to pull her mood together.

"Hey, Lori. You look great. I love the color of that sweat shirt. The blue really brings out your eyes. Did you have a chance to get some breakfast?"

"Yes, I did." Maybe she had misjudged him. After all, a guy who seemed to be so nice to Mark and so considerate toward her couldn't be *too* slimy—could he? "Well, I'm ready."

"Okay, then. Off we go." With a friendly smile, Frank went to the door and held it open for Lori, who was starting to feel a little guilty about the way she thought about him. Maybe she had blown everything out of proportion about this whole field trip. Maybe Frank just acted weird because he was insecure or something. . . .

Inside Frank's black Chevy Nova, he handed her a map. He'd already drawn a circle around Oakdale, their destination. "Here, Lori. You want to see where we're going? This way you'll know when I'm leading you astray." He winked at her, and Lori shook her head with a laugh. "Actually, there are a couple of places where you might have to tell me where to turn—my dad always drives and I usually sleep."

"I'll try to help," Lori agreed, hoping she wouldn't get them lost. That would be the

worst— *Hey!* thought Lori suddenly. *Maybe
that's just what Frank has in mind.* She shook
the thought off at once. *Don't be paranoid,* she
told herself as she smoothed out the map on
her lap. The car made its way to the rolling
hills on the other side of Merivale.

"My mother said something about snow
later today, so we should probably keep it
short," Lori said when they reached the junc-
tion of Route 73 and Main Street. Even with
the heat on in the car, Lori could still see her
breath.

"No problem. When you want to go, just
let me know," Frank replied.

For the first time, Lori finally relaxed.
She decided Frank wasn't so bad after all—
his manner was just a bit obnoxious, that was
all.

As they slowly climbed the foothills, they
left the suburban sprawl of developments and
shopping malls. These were replaced by small
clapboard farmhouses, outbuildings, and dead
trees that pierced the heavy overcast sky with
their spiky branches. The small farms were
like oases in the acres of barren, just-har-
vested fields.

Soon even these outposts disappeared as
they moved up into the mountains. Lori
felt suddenly exhilarated about being in the
countryside.

After an hour more of climbing, they came

to a fork in the road. Route 73 officially ended and narrowed into two roads.

"Okay, Lori, what's next?" asked Frank.

Quickly consulting her map, Lori determined the best route to Oakdale. "Bear right—that's got to be Stony Ridge Lane."

"Are you sure?" he asked, sounding confused. "It doesn't seem right. Let me take a look."

Frank pulled the car over to the side of the road and slid across the seat until he was leaning against Lori. Glancing at the map, he found Stony Ridge Lane and traced an imaginary route with his left index finger. As he did so, his right arm began casually creeping over Lori's shoulders. Soon, he was stroking the ends of her hair.

"Hey! What are you doing?" asked Lori.

"Nothing," he replied innocently. "Just being friendly—that's all." With that, his fingers found the neckline of her red woolen jacket.

"Cut it out," Lori said, pushing his hand away. "In case you forgot, I already have a boyfriend. His name is Nick Hobart."

Frank shrugged and leaned back in toward her. "Come on, Lori. Just because you have a boyfriend doesn't mean you and I can't—well, be friends. You're so pretty—"

Oh, boy. Frank O'Conner was about two inches away from trying to kiss her.

"Of course we can be friends, but that's it. Now, scoot back to your side of the car, and we'll forget all this." Lori gently nudged him away.

"Oh, Lori, I've just got to—" His eyes were closed and his lips were coming in for a landing. Lori took a deep breath and jerked her head out of the way. At the same time she slammed her hand down on the door handle and slid gracefully out of the car. Frank fell and now lay sprawled along the seat, his arms dangling out the open door.

"Cut it out, Frank! I mean it. Stop!" *What a jerk!* Lori was breathing hard, and little white puffs of warm air punctuated each of her words. She knew Frank was a creep, but she didn't think he would stoop this low.

Frank pulled himself up, hunched his shoulders, and started to say something, but thought better of it. He lowered his eyes and shot Lori an angry glare before sliding over to his side of the car. He gripped the steering wheel tightly, and started the engine as Lori climbed back in. She concentrated on looking out her window, and for the next half-hour they said not one word to each other.

"Here we are," he announced, pulling up to a small log cabin set just off the road in the midst of deep pine and hemlock woods.

Lori was steaming. She didn't think they were actually going to the cabin! Oh, well, she could take care of herself, she knew. She stared at the porch that ran the entire length of the cabin. There were pumpkins set in a pile beside the top step, and flanking the door were two rustic cane-backed rockers. It was lovely but she didn't want to give Frank the satisfaction of telling him so. He'd probably take that as a sign that she wanted to be more than his friend or something.

"Listen, Lori," he said sheepishly. "I'm sorry about what happened before. Can we just declare a truce for the rest of the day?"

Softening a little, Lori looked over at him. He really did look sincere, and she guessed anybody could make a mistake.

"Okay," she agreed, giving him the benefit of the doubt.

"This place has been in the family for ages," Frank explained as they began walking up the gravel path toward the house. "My grandfather built it."

"It's very nice," Lori admitted. No sense holding a grudge either.

Frank opened the door and the two stepped into the cabin. Even though it was cold outside, it felt cozy. Lori blew on her hands and looked around.

The walls were the cut side of the same logs the cabin was built from. At all the windows were checked cotton valances, and the furniture was made of oak and was from the turn of the century. A large stone fireplace stood in the center of the main room. It was lovely, but Lori thought she could have done without the stuffed moose staring down at her from over the mantel.

"My dad does a lot of hunting. Last year he bagged a bear." Frank pointed to a photo of Frank's dad standing over one dead bear.

Lori cringed. Hunting was definitely not her thing. "Oh," she finally managed to comment.

Suddenly Frank's arm was around her shoulder. "Don't worry, I'll protect you," he promised.

Lori pulled away abruptly. Frank seemed to be up to his old tricks again. "Think I'd rather have the bears protect me from you," she said very pointedly. "So where's the algae? Let's get started."

With a frown, Frank led her to the back door, which opened onto a deck. "There's a pond about a half mile in," he said. "Right down that path."

"Well, let's go," said Lori. She stepped onto the deck and stared out at the woods. She didn't know which was worse, the dense forest filled with wild animals in front of her—or Frank at her back.

CHAPTER FOUR

"You call this half a mile?"

Frank turned and grinned at her. "Sorry. I'm not very good at distances."

It was more like two miles, thought Lori as they finally arrived at the pond, which, fortunately, was not frozen over.

For the better part of an hour, Frank stood by, supervising and pointing out likely spots for collection, while Lori did most of the actual dirty work of bagging the specimens and getting her boots soaked through in the process. Lori would have demanded that he help her, but she just wanted to get the collecting over and done with. Heavy gray clouds had slowly been gathering all day, and she didn't want to be caught in a storm.

"I'm pooped," Lori said finally at about two. "How about lunch?"

Frank brought out the sandwiches Lori's mother had prepared, and they ate—Lori quickly, wanting to get started home, Frank taking his sweet time. "There're one or two more places I think we should try on the other side of the pond," he suggested when he finally finished eating.

"Listen, Frank, we've got enough. I'd like to get home if you don't mind. My feet are freezing, and if I don't catch pneumonia, it'll be a miracle."

"Hey, Lori, you want to get an A on this project, don't you?" Frank asked innocently. "What's the point of coming all the way up here if we don't take full advantage of the opportunity?"

Now, what does he mean by that, Lori wondered. Everything Frank said seemed to have two meanings.

"Oh, all right, but just for another half-hour," she agreed reluctantly. "But this time, how about *helping* me collect the stuff?"

"I'd love to, Lori," said Frank apologetically, "but the smell of it makes me gag, know what I mean?"

So saying, he wiped his mouth with a napkin and got up, leading her onward, farther around the pond. Following behind him, Lori looked up and noticed that the clouds were growing darker by the minute. She hunched herself deeper into her jacket and flipped her collar up.

By the time they had finished and found their way back to the cabin, light snow was beginning to fall. The feeble light was fading fast, and a chill wind blew hard against their backs as they walked up to the car. Lori could barely feel her toes anymore, and her hands weren't faring much better. She put the specimens into the back seat and closed the door. *It's a good thing I dressed for winter*, she mused, slapping her hands together.

She caught Frank looking as if he were ready to spring at her. "No, Frank," she told him before he had a chance to say a word. "You *don't* have to hold my hand to keep me warm."

Frank held his arms out, protesting his innocence. "Did I say anything?" he demanded.

"Just take me home," she said, climbing into the car. Frank started the car and turned the heat on before he ran back and locked up the cabin. It was snowing hard now, blowing horizontally as he pulled the car onto the road.

Frank turned on the car radio. "And to repeat, the first severe storm of the season is rapidly approaching the Oakdale area. Expect accumulations of at least a foot. Three inches have already fallen along East Ridge. Motorists are advised to use extreme caution because of slippery road conditions. Stay tuned for further updates—"

"Where's East Ridge?" asked Lori, beginning to feel nervous.

"About two miles up ahead," said Frank, concerned. "Maybe we shouldn't go on, Lori," he suggested. "This is going to be a dangerous drive."

Lori sat bolt upright. If they drove right then, they'd be all right. No more chances for him to get her alone. "Huh-uh!" she insisted. "No way. We're going home now and that's that. Just drive carefully, and slowly."

Frank's jaw tightened. "Whatever you say," he replied grimly, rubbing at the fogged-up windshield.

They crept along for a couple of miles. Lori felt guiltier by the minute for insisting on braving it through the storm. The windshield wipers barely kept up with the accumulation. If they wound up in a ditch, it would be all her fault.

Suddenly, they spotted the revolving red light of a patrol car through the white curtain of snow just ahead. When they got closer, they saw that a van had skidded off the road and down into a gully.

Frank rolled down his window and called to the police officer. "Was anyone hurt?"

"No, fortunately," the officer answered. "Could have been worse—the roads are pretty impassable. Where you headed?"

"Merivale," Frank told him.

"Merivale? Forget it," the trooper responded, shaking his head. "All the roads are closed between here and Route Seventy-three. I'm afraid you'll have to turn around. I'd advise you to get to shelter as quick as you can. This one's turning into a blizzard, and fast!"

Lori couldn't believe her ears. *This is a nightmare!* she said to herself. They could be killed or they could die from exposure. But then, she wondered, would that be worse than being stranded in the middle of nowhere with Frank O'Conner?

Danielle regarded her mirror with a sly smile. Her outfit was perfect for a date with Don James. She was wearing a black leather miniskirt, a black cashmere turtleneck, a bold silver pendant, and an oversize gray jacket cut like a man's with the sleeves rolled up. Not exactly what she'd wear to go out with an Atwood boy, but this night was something different—and so was Don.

Dousing herself with Fallen Angel, she purposely tousled her amazing red hair and followed this with a spritz of copper mousse.

Feeling daring, Danielle checked her digital clock. Seven-twenty. She was late. Perfect. It was always good to keep a date waiting, just a little. Grabbing the keys to her BMW and slinging her fox jacket over her shoulder, she ran downstairs to her father's study.

"Dad, I'm going."

Mike Sharp looked up from the blueprints he was poring over and raised an eyebrow. "Who's the lucky guy, Danielle?" he asked.

"Oh, just a kid—" she responded vaguely. Her father wouldn't even know who Don James was, but still—

"Well, have a good time," her father said vaguely, blowing a quick kiss in her direction.

"Mike! I told you we're due at the Martins at eight!" Serena Sharp's voice cut into their private moment. Appearing beside Danielle a moment later, Danielle's mother was a dazzling vision in a strapless ivory evening dress with diamond earrings and brooch—except for the scowl on her face.

"Oh, hi, Danielle. Are you going out tonight?" her mother asked as she fidgeted with her diamond bracelet.

"Yes, to the movies."

"Well, have a nice time, honey. Come on, Mike, I'm really getting annoyed." She let the annoyance sound in her voice. "It's black tie, you know, and you're not even dressed!"

Danielle sighed and backed away from her parents. "I'll see you, guys," she called.

"Right, dear," her mother answered without much interest. It was amazing how quickly her parents could bring Danielle down. They were just so busy, so wrapped up in themselves, and so indifferent that Danielle sometimes wanted to scream: *Look at me! I'm here!* But most of the time her way of dealing with their indifference was just to numb out whenever she was around them.

The click of the door closing behind her then was like music. That night she'd be far from the wealthy world of Wood Hollow Hills and Atwood Academy.

Danielle slid into the glove leather front seat of her car and checked herself out once again in the mirror. The peach lipstick was supreme. Turning the radio to WMER, the local rock station, she began her journey to the other side of town to pick up Don.

"A travelers' advisory is in effect tonight in the mountains due west of Merivale because of an early-season snowstorm. If you're in the valley, carry an umbrella—there'll be rain, and it could be heavy at times. And now let's listen to the Golden Ponies' latest release, 'Chained Love.' You heard it on WMER. Come on, rock me, baby!" The DJ's voice faded and the driving beat of a rock song came on fast and furious. A little smile crept over Danielle's face. She felt freer than she had in months as she drove the rest of the way to Don's.

A row of Harley motorcycles lined up in the driveway of Don's place was the first thing to catch Danielle's eye. The sagging porch was the second. No way was she going to set foot in that house.

Honk! Honk! Danielle hoped Don wouldn't keep her waiting too long, and he didn't. She hadn't been there two minutes before she saw him step out of the house, hatless, in the light drizzle that had just begun.

With a smile and a wink, he sauntered over to her car and swung the passenger door open. "Hey, Red—you actually made it," he said, leaning in.

Was she imagining it, or did he sound surprised? "Of course I made it. We do have a date, don't we?"

"Well, yeah, but you never know with you rich girls. . . ." Don threw her a meaningful look with his dark, mysterious eyes, and she couldn't help staring at his handsome face for a moment. In the glow from the interior light, his chiseled features and strong jaw made her heart flip.

"Too bad about the rain," he said, turning up the collar of his leather jacket. "I thought we could take a little ride on the Harley, but maybe next time, huh?"

Next time? There couldn't ever be a next time, of course—this was a one-time-only adventure. Danielle knew it was sheer madness to go out with Don even once. But there she was—there *they* were, *together*. Well, almost, anyway. Why didn't he get in? "Hop in," she said coyly. "Maybe I'll let you drive on the way back."

"So, where we going, Red?" he said as he slid in, stretching out to make himself comfortable. "Don't worry," he said. "I had myself dry-cleaned so I wouldn't soil the upholstery."

Danielle smiled to be polite, but she was having trouble concentrating on what he was saying. The rich smell of his leather jacket mingling with his after shave had her emotions in a turmoil. Why couldn't the Atwood guys she usually went out with be a little more like Don, she wondered.

"Is that all you're wearing?" asked Danielle, indicating the leather jacket. "They're predicting a lot of rain later."

"That's okay, Red. I've got my love to keep me warm." He winked and settled against the leather upholstery. "Well, where we going?"

Backing out of the driveway, Danielle looked both ways to avoid the motorcycles and Don's long white T-bird. "I was thinking a movie might be fun," she suggested.

"Then a movie it is," he replied. "The SixPlex?"

No way! On a Saturday night half of Atwood Academy would be at the SixPlex. Sure, she was out with Don James just for fun, but that didn't mean she was about to commit social suicide.

"Actually," Danielle purred, "I thought the Westview Art Cinema would be better—no lines."

"I'll say—no lines, no popcorn, and no seats that aren't broken," he murmured. "But best of all, no chance of running into any of your fancy friends from the 'academy.' " Don chuckled softly when he said that.

That caught Danielle by surprise. How could he possibly know that was the real reason she wanted to go all the way across town? She glanced over at Don, but he was looking out the window, humming tunelessly.

"Don't be dumb," she said. He turned and cocked an eyebrow at her. "I don't care who we run into," she insisted a bit too strongly. "It's just that *Bold Fire* is playing there, and you know that Jeremy Simons got his start in it."

"Well, I'm game," replied Don.

A British film would probably be way over Don's head, but what else could they do? "It starts at nine, so we have plenty of time," said Danielle with a glance at her dashboard clock.

"Great," he replied, not taking his eyes off her as she drove along the rainy streets, the windshield wipers ticking softly. He didn't say a thing, but Danielle could feel his eyes boring into her—she was practically on fire.

Didn't he know he was driving her crazy! Nervously tapping the steering wheel, Danielle finally turned and met his eyes. They were passing under a street light, and his face was lit up for that second. He grinned long and slow at her. He *did know* the effect he was having on her. The *rat*!

He started to laugh then, great side-splitting bellows, and soon she had to join in with the infectious sound. He always knew just when and how to lighten any situation.

When they pulled into the parking lot, they both had tears rolling down their cheeks. Don opened up his car door and got out. Danielle waited for him to come around and open her door, but he just stood there grinning at her, the rain dripping down his face. Finally, she opened her door and ran to shelter in a doorway.

"It's early. Want a Coke?" he asked, walking up and joining her. He shook his head like a wet dog and scattered raindrops on Danielle.

A delicious shiver made its way up Danielle's spine and back down again. She laughed once more and delighted in being with him. But she had to decide about the Coke. There was a diner across the street, but it was always crowded. Just in case some of the other Atwood kids were slumming it, she decided that she had better stay away.

"Um—actually, I'd like to pick up some nail polish from the drugstore, if you don't mind."

"Now?" Don looked confused.

"Yes, it's urgent. I'm all out of Perfectly Pink, and I can't really live without it," she said, making fun of herself a little.

Don raised his eyebrows and gently took hold of her hand. He lifted her fingers and inspected them. "They look 'perfectly' fine to me."

Danielle giggled and withdrew her hand. Her hand in his felt just too intense.

"What's the matter, Red? Am I making you nervous?"

"Don't be silly," Danielle insisted, boldly taking his hand again. She was never going to see Don James again, so why not go for it? "Come on."

Danielle led Don across the parking lot to Brady's Drugs. She quickly surveyed the store to make sure no one she knew was there. When she was sure the coast was clear, she dragged him over to the nail polish section and searched the rack for her shade.

"Here it is," he said, deftly picking it up off the display. "Perfectly awful, if you ask me. You ever try doing without this junk, Red? You don't need all this makeup and stuff, you know. Not with your looks."

Danielle's fair complexion turned bright red from her forehead to her chin. What was happening to her? She knew she was great-looking, millions of people had already told her so, so why did he have such an effect on her?

He put the polish in her palm, closed her fingers around it, then held her hand in his and looked down into her eyes. Neither of them moved.

"Come on, let's get our picture taken," Don finally said, breaking the spell. Still holding her hand, Don headed for the photo booth next to the lipsticks.

"Oh, I don't know—" she objected.

"It'll be fun. And I'll have something to remember you by."

Danielle gave him a look that was half smile, half pout. "But those things always make me look terrible!"

"Impossible. Come on!"

Before she knew it, she was behind the curtain sharing a tiny stool with him.

"Come on, loosen up!" he said, mussing her hair and tickling her ribs.

"Don!" she screamed with a laugh.

Snap!

"Here we go again—" This time Don put his arm around her shoulder, wrestler-style. Danielle was giggling like crazy when the flash went off.

They tried a serious pose, but at the last minute he said, "Watch the birdie!" and she lost it again.

"Wait a minute!" cried Danielle, turning to him after the third picture. Gently reaching up to his forehead, she moved a stray lock of still wet hair that had fallen onto his forehead, and their eyes locked. The snap of the photo machine caught the intensity of that tender look on film.

"We look great together, no doubt about it—here's the proof, Danielle—look."

Danielle—he had called her by her name instead of his usual teasing nickname of Red. And—and the sound of her name on his lips was sheer heaven. Danielle could feel herself melting.

But forcing herself to glance down at her watch, she saw that it was a quarter to nine already. Where had the time gone? They were going to be late for the movie. Not that it really mattered. It was sure to be boring—

unless Don intended to spice up the next two hours in the dark.

"Come on!" she cried, reshelving the polish and grabbing his arm to lead him out the door.

Minutes later, breathless from running, they were settling into their seats at the movie. Don took her hand again, and this time it felt so comfortable, so right. *Just for tonight*, Danielle told herself with a smile plastered over her face. *Just for tonight*. And with that, the lights dimmed down all around them, fading into darkness. . . .

CHAPTER FIVE

By the time Lori and Frank made it back to the cabin, it was pitch-dark. Frank had to leave the headlights on while he and Lori cleared an immense snowdrift from the front steps leading up to the porch.

Lori was freezing. Her fingers ached and her feet were numb. She wished she were home, curled up in her toasty-warm bed with a cup of hot cocoa. She was angry with herself too. How could she have been so dumb? How had she managed to fall victim to Frank's wild scheme in the first place? She couldn't stand the idea that she was going to be marooned with him—*all night long*. Still, after that nightmare of a drive, the little cabin in the woods was a welcome sight.

"Where's the light switch?" she asked as she searched the wall with her fingers.

"There aren't any," Frank answered with a shrug.

"Then how do you turn on the lights?" she wondered out loud.

"We don't have electricity," he said matter-of-factly. "Dad is one of those back-to-nature freaks."

"Come on, Frank. I'm too exhausted for jokes."

"I'm not kidding. Sorry, Lor—"

Lori suddenly realized he was serious. "What are we going to use for light then? Candles?"

"What do we need light for?" he asked obnoxiously. "I kind of like it dark."

"Frank O'Conner, when are you going to give up! Things are bad enough now—we could be stuck here for days!"

His shifty green eyes twinkled. "Yeah, if we get lucky."

Lori stiffened. "That does it."

"Oh, come on, Lori. I was only kidding," he said. "We have camping lanterns. They work with kerosene. Watch." Pulling some matches out of his pocket and lighting one, he walked over to a strange-looking glass thing on a table in the living room, and lit its wick. A bright white flame instantly appeared. "Not bad, huh? They're all over the cabin."

The lanterns were nice, Lori thought. But she wouldn't admit it to Frank.

Suddenly, another thought occurred to Lori. "Don't tell me—we don't have any heat, right?"

"Nope, we don't." Frank grinned. In the light of the lanterns, his expression was positively devilish. "This fireplace heats the house good enough. It's very warm—and very romantic."

"Oh, please," groaned Lori. "Look, while you're stoking it up, why don't I call home? Where's the phone?"

"About three miles down the road at the nearest diner," Frank said offhandedly, breaking up a handful of kindling.

Lori stopped dead in her tracks. "There's no phone either?"

"If you don't believe me, see for yourself," he said, sounding a little offended. "Honestly, Lori, you act like I planned the whole blizzard just to get you up here all alone."

Lori huffed. "You know something, I wouldn't be the least bit surprised," she muttered grumpily.

Lori knew it wasn't really Frank's fault that they'd been caught in the storm. She just wished she'd never agreed to come in the first place. She knew her parents would be worried sick, and Nick would be too. If only she could call them all to explain.

Frank lit a match to the beautifully laid fire. It filled the living room with a soft reddish glow almost immediately. At least he could do *something* right, Lori decided. She sat down near the hearth, running her fingers through her damp hair so the warmth could dry it out. She was happy to be feeling a little warmer, but she wished Frank would go away.

He crouched down beside her. "Would you like to get out of those wet clothes?" he asked.

"Not on your life," Lori said sternly.

Frank looked downright offended. "You don't always have to be so suspicious, you know."

"I suppose you don't know about your reputation?" Lori shot back sarcastically.

Frank smiled. "Sometimes a reputation is better than the truth," he said, giving her a meaningful look.

Lori was startled. Could it be that Frank deliberately cultivated his reputation just so people wouldn't know the truth about him? And what was the truth?

"Wait here," said Frank, going off into the bedroom. Lori stared after him, not sure what to think now.

In a moment he returned with some

woolen socks, a pair of old jeans, and a blue plaid flannel shirt. "Matches your eyes," he said, holding up the shirt for her approval. "Is it okay?"

What was it with him? He actually did something kind without wanting anything in return? *Is it possible he's a decent guy after all?* Lori was very grateful to have something warm and dry to wear.

"It's fine. Thanks," she replied.

"I've got to get out of these things too. I smell like swamp water." Frank stood up and started to strip his sweater off.

"Hey! Wait a minute! What are you doing?" she asked incredulously.

"Changing," he answered casually.

Lori sprang to her feet. "I'll go into a bedroom, if you don't mind." Marching inside, she locked the door behind her. Maybe Frank wasn't all bad, but she still didn't trust him.

In the bedroom Lori took off her soggy sweat shirt and put on the blue plaid shirt. It was at least four sizes too large, and so were the jeans, but she didn't care. The woolen socks soothed her cold, red feet. She was comfortable and that was all that mattered right then. She glanced into the mirror, smoothed some stray hairs around her face, and laughed. She knew she looked ridiculous.

When she emerged, Frank was bent over

the fireplace, holding the handle of a frying pan. "Dinner will be served very soon," he announced. "Hope you like canned food."

"Mmmm—" said Lori, plopping down. Lunch seemed to have been an eternity ago, and just looking at the food made her mouth water.

"You must be hungry—here." Frank put a generous portion of baked beans on her plate. "I don't want you to starve."

"Thanks," she said, taking the plate.

"You're welcome," he replied simply—for a change. With a smile, he raised a glass of apple juice to her and drank.

He really is handsome, thought Lori, glancing at his even features and sharp green eyes in the dancing firelight. Not anyone she could ever really go for, but he was handsome and he was trying to act nice.

"You know something? Baggy suits you," Frank said with a wry smile.

Lori let out a laugh. "Oh, come on—now I *know* you're crazy."

"Admit it, Lori, you're madly in love with me, right?"

Lori rolled her eyes. "You know, you'd actually be okay if you'd just ease off a bit. I bet you could even get yourself a girl friend someday. You should try being a human being more often. It suits you."

"Ah, Lori let's face it. You bring out the

best in me. If I had a girl like you around, I could really be a nice guy," he answered, giving her a meaningful look.

"Forget it, Frank. Really. I already have a boyfriend. If you're lonely, there are lots of girls around. Maybe if you showed them your better side, they'd give you a try."

Frank seemed annoyed. "Lonely? Give me a break! I'm not lonely!"

From his reaction, Lori knew she had hit the truth right on the head. So that was why Frank acted like such a dork—he *was* lonely. She almost felt sorry for him.

Finishing the last of her beans, Lori found herself yawning. "Well, I don't know about you, but I'm ready for bed."

Frank put his hand on hers. "Me too," he said, his eyes large and liquid.

"Quit it, will you!" Lori laughed as she got up. Now that she knew he was ninety percent put-on, she wasn't worried about him anymore. Well, not *too* much anyway.

"I was only kidding, really. I'll sleep out here on the sofa. You can take the bedroom."

Lori went into the little bedroom, closing and locking the door behind her. She had just pulled the covers over her and gotten comfortable, when she heard Frank's knock.

"Now what?" she demanded.

"You'd better leave your door open," he advised her.

"Why in the world would I do a stupid thing like that?"

"Because if you don't, you'll freeze. The fire's out here, remember?"

Defeated, Lori went to the door and opened it. Frank was standing there, smiling at her. "Good night, gorgeous," he said softly.

Lori turned without a word and climbed into bed, fully clothed. She rested her head on the pillow, but didn't bother to close her eyes. It was useless. Even if he wasn't all bad, she knew that she'd never sleep a wink with Frank in the next room.

To Danielle, *Bold Fire* was just a disconnected series of images and characters talking about things she only vaguely understood. She was bored as could be right after the opening credits were finished, because she couldn't seem to follow the action of the film. If only they could have gone to the SixPlex and seen something really terrific, but that would have been much too risky.

Danielle spent most of the movie glancing over at Don. She thought he'd be wearing the same bored expression that she was, but she was wrong. Don's face was a study of concentration. He was actually enjoying the movie! But how could he be?

Not once did he even try to put his arm around her. More and more frustrated, Dan-

ielle even thought about walking out on him.
How dare he ignore her! They didn't come to
an art movie to watch it, surely?

When the movie was finally over, Danielle
was steaming. She stood up to go immediately, but Don pulled her back. "Let's wait
for the crowd to thin out," he whispered
somewhat ironically. There were only about
thirty other people in the entire theater.
Danielle thought he might finally make a move
for her, but when she turned to look at him,
he had a thoughtful expression on his face.
He was actually reading all the names of the
people who had made the movie.

"Great flick," he said at last, pulling his
leather jacket from the back of his chair.

Danielle reached for her new fox and
turned to him with a pout. "I thought it was
pretty weird, actually."

"You don't go in for avant-garde stuff,
huh, Red?"

"You *do*?" she asked, so surprised that
she forgot to be mad at him.

"Well, I like most of this director's stuff,
and I thought the dream images were pretty
sensational."

So that's what those weird sections were,
Danielle realized. In that case, the movie might
actually have made a lot of sense. Danielle
looked over at Don. Maybe she'd been seriously underestimating him all this time. . . .

"When she was running through that corn field, I thought that was great. And then that time when he tried to show her being two places at once . . . Those are the kinds of things that make great films." Don was so involved in talking about the movie that he didn't take her hand or put his arm around her when they walked out of the theater. Danielle was so enthralled by this new side of Don that she didn't even mind.

Out in the parking lot, where it had stopped raining, Danielle tried to keep up with him by throwing in a few semi-intelligent comments just to let him know she wasn't stupid.

"Well, that flick was a great idea, Red— you really know how to pick 'em." With that, Don threw a muscular arm around her neck and pulled her close. She found herself curling into the smooth leather of his jacket as they walked. She felt almost dizzy being so close to him. Her face was flushed, and she couldn't stop smiling. She pulled back from him for a second to look up into his clear, bright eyes.

He grinned back at her, without a care. "YA-HOO!" he yelled. "This is *some girl!*"

"Look who's there!" The girl's voice far behind them was dreadfully familiar to Danielle. She didn't have to turn around to know it was Teresa Woods.

"It *is* Danielle, Teresa. You're right!" came a second familiar voice across the whole parking lot.

Oh, no! Heather Barron too! What in the world were they doing at the Westview? "Danielle!" called Teresa.

Danielle froze, desperate to find a way out. "Come on, Don. Run—" she whispered.

"What's going on?" he wanted to know, turning around and searching the lot with his eyes. He must have been concentrating on Danielle so hard that he hadn't even heard the other girls calling her.

"Oh, nothing. Don't turn around and look! It's just some girls. They're from Atwood and they're always bothering me for a lift home." It sounded like a pretty thin lie to Danielle, and she was hoping against hope that he wouldn't see through it.

Don nodded, and broke into a run. "Let's go then," he said, grabbing her hand to pull her along.

When they got to the car, they jumped in and hid in the front seat. If Danielle fired up the engine and tore out of the parking lot, they'd know it was her for sure. There weren't many white BMWs in town. She sat up a bit later and nervously checked the rearview mirror, but she didn't see Teresa or Heather anymore. Could she really lie later and tell them she'd been someplace else? She had to convince them, or else it was all over.

Danielle drove back toward Don's place feeling sick to her stomach. Her entire life, everything she'd worked for at Atwood, would be totally ruined if Teresa and Heather had seen Don.

"Hey, Red, relax. Everything'll be okay— these things have a way of working out, you know." Don reached over and took her hand, and Danielle couldn't help but feel a little better. Without being told what was happening, he knew. And he hadn't made fun of her or put her down in any way. In fact, he didn't even seem to be hurt.

Maybe he was right too. After all, it was pitch-black in the parking lot, and Teresa and Heather had been kind of far away from them. Maybe they didn't really know it was Danielle. Maybe they were only guessing. Maybe they hadn't recognized Don. Even if they had, maybe she could deny it.

Maybe. Maybe . . . But, Danielle knew, maybes didn't count now. Maybes weren't going to get her out of this one. She had only herself—and, she decided, that really wasn't so bad. After all, she was Danielle Sharp!

CHAPTER SIX

The next morning, Lori slammed the front door of her house with a thud. "Hello. I'm home!" she yelled. She knew her parents must have been frantic with worry. Lori felt relief as Frank's car screeched out of the driveway. Thank goodness it was Sunday and she'd have a whole day without him. Their next meeting was in bio, and it seemed a million years away.

When no one came to meet her right away, Lori reached down and picked up a shopping bag full of clanking jars. Very carefully, she walked with them to the back porch. The last thing she needed was for a quart of swamp water to spill on the carpet. *Good old Frank*, Lori muttered as she took the jars out of the bag and placed them next to Mark's baseball gear. Not only had he completely ruined her weekend, but he'd also stuck her with most of the analyzing of the goop they'd collected. Rather than spend the extra time with him, she had volunteered to write up the lab report too.

"Lori!" Her mother ran out on the porch and hugged her. When she pulled back, Lori could see that her mother hadn't slept at all the night before. Her eyes were red-rimmed and her skin was pale. The expression on her face was downright alarmed.

Fast on her heels came Lori's father. He was breathing hard, and he had the same worried look.

"What happened to you, for heaven's sake?" he wanted to know. "Did you realize how worried your mother—"

Lori couldn't tell if he was angry or just upset.

"Wait, George. Let me handle this," Lori's mother interrupted. She walked into the kitchen with her arm still around Lori's waist. All three of them took chairs at the round table. "Now, honey, what happened? We were naturally upset with you gone all night."

"I understand that you would be," said Lori. "We got caught in the storm. And had to spend the night at a cabin Frank's parents have, and that's all that happened."

"Now, Lori—you know I trust you—but—" said her mother.

"We don't know this boy!" declared her father.

"And when his parents called to ask if you'd made it back here—" said her mother.

"Honestly, we just got snowed in. I would have called, but there was no phone. And we couldn't get to one. Actually, we did try coming back last night, but the troopers told us to turn back. So we spent the night at the cabin and came back the first thing in the morning. That's all," explained Lori.

Mr. Randall looked suspicious. "That's all? And you couldn't get to a phone this morning?" His voice seemed heavy with meaning.

"I'm sorry, Daddy, I just didn't think to call on the way home. I just wanted to get here."

There was an awful silence for a few minutes before her mother broke it. "Are you *sure* nothing happened in that cabin, Lori? I want you to be honest with me—it's very important."

Hot tears of humiliation suddenly sprang into Lori's eyes as she realized exactly what her parents were thinking.

"I don't even like Frank very much. And nothing happened in that cabin! Nothing! I ate a plate of canned beans and then I went to bed.

"Honestly, it was all a big nothing," Lori sputtered. "Listen, I've got to get some sleep. I didn't get a wink last night because I was so upset and worried. But what could I do? Get a pair of skis and head back to Merivale? I was in an impossible situation!"

"All right, honey—get some sleep," murmured Lori's mother. "But first, come get another hug."

Lori clung to her mother for a minute and then gave her dad a quick kiss before heading to her room. The minute she left she heard her father say, "I don't like it, Cynthia, not one bit."

And her mother answered, "She's a good girl, and if she says nothing happened— nothing happened."

Flopping down on the bed, Lori knew her parents had a right to be upset. After all, she'd spent the entire night alone with a boy— that sounded pretty heavy—unless they'd actually been there, of course.

Well, at least it was all over now. She'd never have to spend another minute alone with Frank O'Conner, and she could call Nick and explain. He might not like what had happened, but at least he'd believe her.

Lori glanced at her clock. Ten thirty-five. No sense calling him now. Most Sundays he

and his family visited his grandmother in a
neighboring town. If only she knew his grandmother's last name, but she was on his mother's side of the family. Images of the pond
and of Nick blended together in her mind
until she drifted into sleep and began dreaming. . . . She was swimming in a pond with
Nick on a beautiful summer's day—Mr. Harris was there, too, collecting algae. . . .

Something unusual was happening in Lori's Monday-morning art class. Every so often
she had the feeling that someone was staring
at her. It was strange. She'd look up, but
she'd never catch anyone's eye. Lori began to
feel jumpy. Maybe, she decided, it was just
an aftereffect of her unnerving weekend with
Frank O'Conner. If only she could talk to
Patsy or Ann right then. She knew she could
count on them to help her sort things out.

When the bell rang, Lori headed down
the hall to the cafeteria. That was strange.
Stu Henderson just smiled and waved at her—
she was sure he didn't like her. There was
Tom Darrell, smiling at her too. And she'd
never even spoken to him. Hey, what was
wrong? Mary Ryan and Betsy McCall just
ignored her completely. *What is going on? Or
am I just being paranoid?*

"Yoo-hoo!" That high, piercing voice
could only belong to Gina Nichols, Merivale

High's head cheerleader. Catching up to Lori just outside the cafeteria, Gina was grinning from ear to ear. "I heard you had quite a weekend." Gina giggled. "Was it fun?"

Now Lori knew something was up. Gina Nichols never spoke to her—in fact, Gina actively disliked Lori. "You mean collecting algae?" News really traveled fast in Merivale High, that was for sure.

"You're too much!" Gina giggled again. "I mean *Frank*. You know, *being* with him. I heard he's a fantastic kisser—is he?"

Lori stopped dead in her tracks. Was Gina implying what she thought she was? She was! What nerve! "How should I know? I was collecting swamp water, not kisses!" She gave Gina a penetrating look, but the cheerleader wasn't put off.

"Oh, come on, Lori—you can talk to *me*."

Gina Nichols had never been one of Lori's favorite people—especially since she'd made Lori's life utterly miserable during the Atwood-Merivale football game. Naturally, Lori's loyalties had been torn then. Nick was the quarterback of the Atwood Cougars, and a lot of people—urged on by Gina—had given Lori a hard time about dating him.

"Excuse me, I'm meeting some of my friends for lunch," said Lori as politely as she could manage.

"Well, you don't have to be so snooty,"

Gina huffed. "A lot of girls wouldn't even talk to you after you spent the weekend alone with a boy. Oh, and by the way, that whole story about it being a biology field trip is pretty lame, Lori."

With that, Gina took off, leaving Lori feeling quite shaken and standing alone in the hall.

The second she entered the cafeteria, she realized the full implication of what was happening. A buzz spread from table to table as she appeared in the cafeteria door, and soon every eye was on her.

Thankfully, Ann and Patsy had already found a table. Without braving the lunch line, Lori went directly to her two friends.

"Whew," said Patsy sympathetically. "Pretty heavy, Lor—"

"Lori, what really happened in the mountains? I know it can't be what they're saying," said Ann, gently touching her friend's arm.

Dazed, Lori sat down and grabbed the edge of the table. "Um—what exactly *are* they saying, Ann? I might as well know the worst."

Ann bit her lip nervously. "That stupid Frank O'Conner. All morning he's been telling anyone and everyone that you spent the night with him alone in his parents' cabin."

"And you know Fast Frankie—there's slime hanging from every word," Patsy chimed in.

"But I *did* spend the night with him. I *had* to. We tried to leave the mountains, but the troopers told us the roads were closed," Lori stammered.

"He didn't mention that part," said Ann dryly. "I guess he was too busy describing your romantic fireside dinner, and how you had to take your clothes off because they were so wet."

"What?" cried Lori furiously. "Oooo—that little twerp!"

"Lori," said Ann softly enough so she wouldn't be overheard, "maybe you'd better have this out with Frank—before it gets worse than it already is."

Lori stood up, her face set and determined. "That's exactly what I'm going to do."

"Frank O'Conner! Just what in the world do you mean by spreading lies about me to everyone in school?"

Frank stared at her as if she were from Mars. "What? I don't know what you're talking about, Lori."

"Tell me you haven't spread it around about our spending the night in the cabin together," she demanded.

"Well, it wasn't my fault," he protested. "The guys dragged it out of me."

"I'm sure," said Lori, rolling her eyes in disgust. "I'll bet you couldn't wait to spread the story all over school. In fact, I wouldn't be surprised if you dreamed up some pretty juicy details just to spice it up. Let's face it, Frank, you wouldn't want to spoil your precious reputation, would you?"

"That's not how it was at all. I promise you."

"Oh, no?"

"As a matter of fact, I made a specific point of telling the guys that, uh, nothing, you know, happened."

"You don't really expect me to believe that, do you?"

"Why not? It's the truth."

"Then why do I keep getting strange looks from boys I don't know? Even freshmen?"

"Beats me. I told the guys a million times, nothing happened—nothing happened . . . I can't help it if they wouldn't believe me!"

Lori looked at Frank, trying to figure out what to believe. She could hear herself telling her parents: "Nothing happened—nothing happened . . ." They had had a hard time believing her—and they were her *parents*!

Lori realized with a shudder that the more she or Frank denied it, the more everyone would believe it.

And if she didn't deny it . . . ? She was dead no matter what she did!

CHAPTER SEVEN

Upstairs on the mall's fourth level, Danielle was busy doing what she did best—shopping. And she was doing it in the place where shopping was the best—Facades, the chicest boutique at Merivale Mall. If Facades didn't have it, it didn't exist.

That Monday, though, shopping was necessary. It was therapy. Just being around the familiar decor was comforting. In a way, Facades was more like home than the house in Wood Hollow Hills because of the tense atmosphere created by her feuding parents.

Danielle considered a pair of teal-colored slacks. No, no good; she already had a pair in that color.

Her whole life was just so depressing.

Forget her parents—they were the least of it. Her status at school was potentially *ruined*!

As for her love life, no matter how much fun she'd had with Don James, she could never, ever see him again. Dating him was just too dangerous.

If she could only find one fantastic item— just one—it might help her forget her Saturday-night disaster. Danielle picked a velvet dress off the rack. It was great, but it had puffy sleeves—too tacky.

By the cool light of Sunday morning, Danielle had pretty well convinced herself that Teresa and Heather really had seen her. *Why do things like this have to happen to me?* Danielle moaned and pulled a peach silk minidress off the rack. Too—peachy . . .

"Isn't there anything else?" Danielle demanded after she'd fingered all the merchandise.

"Well, we did get a shipment of handknit sweaters in from Milan this morning," the saleswoman said. "And I suppose since you're a 'special' customer . . ."

"Yes, I want to see them," Danielle ordered. "I really have to find something super."

"Is there a special occasion, Miss Sharp?" The saleswoman was just being polite, but Danielle took it the wrong way.

"My life," she answered, tossing the woman a superior look.

The saleswoman scurried off in search of the sweaters, and Danielle paced around the store like a restless lioness. That's when she noticed the suede jump suits. Now, *they* were fabulous.

She glanced down at the price tag on one of the suits. A hundred and eighty dollars. For suede, it was a steal. And since she'd just gotten her allowance, she could afford it—no problem.

"Wait, I want to try this first." Danielle pulled two size-seven outfits off the rack, one in gold and one in burgundy. She slipped into the fitting room and quickly tried on the burgundy one. It didn't feel quite right, but she still wanted to see how it looked on her.

Walking out to the antique three-way mirror in the back of the store, Danielle suddenly froze in her tracks. There was Teresa Woods, a mountain of clothes over one arm. Behind her came Heather Barron, her silver bracelets jangling as she pulled a bored hand through her raven hair.

"Danielle! Where were you all day?" Normally, Teresa, Heather, and Danielle hung out as much as they could at school. That day, though, Danielle had feigned a headache so she could sit out any class she shared with Teresa or Heather. And she'd eaten a sandwich in her car for lunch just so she wouldn't run into them in the cafeteria.

Still, she'd known this meeting had to happen sooner or later. Danielle stood up straight and smiled pleasantly. The best defense was a good offense. "Where were *you* is the question? I looked all over for you at lunch." Lying was not so difficult for Danielle as it was for some people. But still, it didn't feel good either.

"Gosh, Danielle," replied Teresa with a devilish grin, "we keep missing each other. At school, at the Westview—"

A hot blush made its way across Danielle's face. She forced her green eyes to widen in surprise. "The Westview?" She said it as if it were another planet—one not named yet.

"Saturday night—*Bold Fire*—" Teresa could hardly suppress her giggling now.

"Huh?" repeated Danielle, desperately searching for a way out.

"We saw you with Don James, Danielle," said Heather levelly.

"Me? And Don James? You must be imagining things. What would I *ever* be doing in a place like the Westview—and with Don James of all people?"

"Oh, walking close, laughing together—" Teresa was enjoying every minute of this.

"That's insane!" Danielle retorted in a huff.

Heather couldn't hold her disbelief in any

more. "Come *on*, Danielle. You can tell us the truth, we're your friends."

"The truth is, you must have seen someone else with Don James," said Danielle.

"Who?" Teresa challenged.

"How should I know?!" Disgusted, Danielle threw her arms in the air.

"Okay, have it your way," Teresa taunted. "If you won't tell us who Don James was out with on Saturday night, we'll just have to ask him ourselves. Come on, Heather. Let's go down to Video Arcade and settle this." With that, Teresa dumped the clothes she'd been holding onto a vacant chair.

They *wouldn't*. They *couldn't*. But there they were, taking off for the arcade. Don would probably be there too. Danielle was in *big* trouble—and she had to do some very fast thinking!

"Lori—that's an enchilada, not a taco." Ernie Goldbloom, the balding, pudgy owner of Tio's, was more concerned than angry. That was the third order Lori had goofed up that day.

"Sorry, Ernie. Let me fix it." Lori took a deep breath and tried to concentrate on her job at Tio's Tacos. It was amazing what a little gossip could do to a person, she thought.

"Lori—wasn't this order to go?"

"Sorry, Isabel," she murmured to Tio's

chef, sixteen-year-old Isabel Vasquez. "Here's
a take-out bag."

"Lori, are you okay?" Isabel asked gin-
gerly. "I heard your parents grounded you
for two months because of Frank and the
cabin." Isabel's brown eyes were full of sincere sympathy.

"What?" answered Lori. "Grounded? No.
My parents weren't really angry. They were
just—upset— I'll tell you all about it later, when
it's less busy." It suddenly occurred to Lori
then that she had never told Isabel a thing
about the weekend. The Merivale grapevine
must really be buzzing!

Whenever she went to the cash register,
Lori could look straight across the promenade of the mall into Hobart Electronics, Nick's
father's store. Sometimes she could catch a
glimpse of Nick if he was working in the
VCR section. But not now. It was too early
for him to be there.

What if he's heard the rumor too? A whole
squadron of butterflies started leaping around
in Lori's stomach. *What if he's furious?*

Lori looked over at Hobart's again, and
this time she saw Nick walking into the store.
Instead of wearing a smile as he usually did,
he was frowning and looking grim.

"Ernie, would you mind if I took my
break now?" She couldn't wait a second longer

to talk to Nick. She had to make him understand.

"I'm sorry, Lori, the dinner crowd will be here any minute." But Ernie could never refuse anybody anything, and he smiled shyly at her. It was that quality of his that inspired so much loyalty among his employees.

"I've got to talk to my boyfriend for a few minutes. It's important," Lori explained.

"You kids—" Ernie was doing his best to be tough. "Ah, go ahead. But be back in fifteen, okay?"

"Thanks a million, Ernie," said Lori.

Lori walked around the central fountain as she made her way across the mall. A couple of kids from Merivale High were sitting on a stone bench talking. Was it her imagination, or did they look at her funny as she passed in front of them? *Don't get paranoid, Randall!* she told herself.

Nick was wrapping up a VCR on the counter near the cash register.

"Nick, hi!" Lori was doing her best to sound worry-free, but she could tell instantly by the look on his face that Nick had already heard about her night with Frank.

Nick seemed to be struggling to control his temper. "Hi, Lori," he responded flatly, ringing up the sale.

"I've been trying to reach you," Lori told him as soon as his customer had walked away.

She stood looking up at him, leaning against the counter that separated them.

"I know. I tried you a few times too."

"Thanks for trying. It was sweet." Nick looked a little embarrassed.

"Can you take a break now so we can talk?"

Nick waved to his dad and pointed to Lori. Mr. Hobart smiled and waved at the two of them, and then he pointed to the door. "Just be back soon," he called out.

Without a word, Nick and Lori went to the back staircase. It led to the underground loading dock, where Nick had first asked Lori out. She noticed that he didn't try to take her hand as he usually would after they'd been apart for so long.

The minute they got downstairs, Nick found a crate and sat down. She took a crate across from him. Their knees were barely touching, and it was a minute before they spoke.

"So?" he said, his aqua eyes meeting hers.

"Well, I guess you've heard some weird stuff about this past weekend." The look in Nick's eyes told her he had. "Listen, Nick. I want you to know that nothing happened. I didn't do anything in that cabin. In fact, I never would have been there at all if a state trooper hadn't ordered us off the road. And that's the honest truth—the whole truth, and nothing but the truth," she added, trying for a little joke.

Nick looked very thoughtful as he drank in every word. "I wasn't going to jump to any conclusions until I heard it from you," he said.

"Well, you just heard it," said Lori, biting her lip. "And I'm so sorry if you were hurt in any way."

"What were you doing there in the first place?" His voice was full of pain.

"We were teamed on a science project. Collecting algae, of all the dumb things. I tried to call and tell you about it. . . ."

Nick was silent.

"I could just strangle that Frank O'Conner," she finally added, steaming. "He's the biggest jerk I ever met." Just looking at Nick was enough to tear Lori up. Did Frank have any idea how many people he'd hurt when he set all this stupid stuff in motion, she wondered.

"Listen, Lor," Nick said finally as he reached over and took her hand. "All this stuff'll blow over. The truth is all that matters."

Lori gazed over at her boyfriend and practically melted. He believed her, trusted her—plain and simple. To Frank, a reputation was better than the truth. To Nick, it was *only* the truth that mattered.

Lori leaned toward Nick and planted a soft, delicate kiss on his lips as she ran her fingers through his golden brown hair. "You're the best," she whispered in his ear. "The absolute best."

"Thanks," he returned, his face relaxing into a smile. "So are you. Now let's just forget all this dumb stuff. Want to go out after work for a little bit?"

"Sure!"

"We can go to O'Burgers and then for a drive, okay?"

"Great!"

As they walked back up the stairs to ground level, Lori sighed with relief. Maybe everything *was* going to be okay. But still, she couldn't shake the nagging suspicion that she hadn't heard the last of Frank O'Conner—or of the nasty rumors that were floating through Merivale.

CHAPTER EIGHT

Her palms sweating, Danielle peered out from the doorway of Facades to where Teresa and Heather were pacing impatiently in front of the glass elevator. Danielle hoped it would never arrive, but even *she* didn't expect to be that lucky. She knew she had to do something drastic, and she had only a few seconds.

Fortunately, her mind worked fast, especially when she was challenged by Teresa. Danielle was nervously looking for a way to beat them down, when a door marked SERVICE STAIRS caught her eye. Without a moment's hesitation, she dashed toward it.

"Miss Sharp! The jump suit!" The saleswoman had followed her out into the corridor. Sure enough, Danielle was still wearing the burgundy jump suit. Quickly snapping

off the price tag, she flung it at the saleswoman and cried, "Put it on my account. I'll
pick up my other stuff later."

Breathless, Danielle ran down the service
stairs—three full flights—her glorious hair
flying behind her.

There was only one thing on her mind—
beating Teresa and Heather to Video Arcade.
If she didn't, her whole life at Atwood would
be ruined.

Every muscle in Danielle's body tensed
when she saw the big red 1 on the gray
service door. She threw it open and flew across
the mall, practically knocking over an older
woman shopper as she ran for Video Arcade.

Scanning the room, she could see that
Teresa and Heather weren't there yet. She'd
made it! Now she had to look for Don. Walking in and out of the rows of machines with
their constant blips, beeps, buzzers, and bells,
Danielle searched every corner. Was it possible that Teresa and Heather had already
come and left—with Don?

No, they hadn't. She breathed heavily.
Off in the corner in the back, the mop of
glossy black hair and broad shoulders stood
out. Don was behind a Star Pirates machine,
blasting away.

"Don!" she cried.

"Hey, Red!" he answered, turning from
his game to give her an appreciative look

from top to bottom. "I had a feeling I might see you here today." Don's smile was almost coy. "What with that electrical storm we had on Saturday—"

He was talking about the feelings between them, and Danielle had to admit to herself that he was right. But there was no way Danielle could let herself fall for his offbeat charm. Not then, and not ever again.

"Don, you've got to help me," she blurted out.

His face turned serious in a second. "What's the matter, Red?"

Thinking fast, she blubbered, "It's my car. It's making all kinds of weird noises." It was a crummy lie, but what else could she do?

"Okay, I'll come take a look at it. Just let me put in one more quarter to zap a few Zork raiders. Then I'll be with you."

"Oh, no, Don!" said Danielle, glancing nervously at the door. "I think you'd better come and check it out right away. I mean, maybe the engine is falling apart as we speak—it really sounds bad! It's parked right near Aunti Pasta's. I've got to go call home and tell them I'll be late. Then I'll meet you up at Facades, okay?"

Danielle could see from the softening in his eyes that her charm was being one hundred percent effective. "All right—BMW have no fear. Big Don is on the way."

"Thanks, Don," she cooed, tossing him the keys. "Would you take it for a spin around the lot—sometimes, it doesn't start making the sound right away." Don shoved his hands in the back pockets of his jeans and sauntered to the door. He stopped for a second and threw her a wink. Danielle started to melt, but stopped when she thought of Don grinding the gears of her new BMW as he burned rubber all over the Merivale Mall lot.

Just as he was safely out of sight, Danielle caught sight of Teresa and Heather, who were scurrying into the arcade. Danielle ducked behind the Star Pirates machine so her friends wouldn't see her and guess she had gotten to Don first.

"I can't believe we got stuck in that dumb elevator for five whole minutes with those nerds from Merivale High." Teresa sounded furious.

Heather looked disgusted. "Wasn't that the worst?"

"I actually thought the short one was going to ask you for a date!" shrieked Teresa, sounding amused now.

Heather was laughing too. "Hey! If it were Danielle, she would have said yes. You know how she goes for those types. Speaking of which—where's Don?"

"If he's not here, he's probably under some car," said Teresa. She and Heather thought that was terrifically funny.

If they only knew it was probably true, Danielle thought as she watched the hysterical giggling.

"He is awfully cute," said Heather, catching her breath. "But *yuck!* I wouldn't be caught dead with him—I'd keep looking for grease stains if he held my hand—"

"Me too," agreed Teresa. "But you know Danielle. Remember a few years ago, her family was no better off than Don James—"

That made Danielle want to explode. She had never been poor, only middle-class. What did she have to do to make her friends forget her humble past?

Danielle sighed. *And people think rich kids have no problems. . . .* She peeked out from behind the Star Pirates machine. *Oh, no—* Teresa and Heather were headed straight for her! When Teresa rested her red alligator bag right on the Pirates machine, Danielle held her breath and crouched down even lower—almost flattening herself against the floor. She didn't move a single muscle.

Heather sighed in defeat. "I guess Don just isn't here."

"We'll get the real story one way or another," Teresa vowed. "I'm practically positive it was her with Don. And we can't let her off the hook. Don will tell us for sure. Come on, let's get out of here."

Danielle's heart was in her throat. She knew Teresa meant business. Even though Danielle was her friend, she was still fair game. And Danielle knew she had to fight back one way or another. It was sink or swim.

Danielle checked the promenade in all directions and ran out the arcade door and back up the service stairs. She took the three flights two steps at a time, at breakneck speed. Then she breezed into Facades and casually strolled around, looking as if she had been there all along.

Perfect, she thought, looking out the window. Teresa and Heather were just getting off the elevator. As they stepped onto the plush maroon carpeting of Facades, Danielle confronted them with a feigned air of confidence. "Now that you two know who Don was out with Saturday night, I hope you'll forget about all this nonsense."

Heather couldn't hide her disappointment. "Don wasn't in the arcade."

"What a pity!" Danielle exclaimed sarcastically.

"You're still not in the clear, Danielle," Teresa warned her, holding up her can of Diet Coke and uncurling one finger to point at Danielle.

"I'm telling you," Danielle insisted, "I

was nowhere near the Westview on Saturday night." Then she paused and did her best to look deeply wounded. "What's the difference? You guys have already condemned me. If you don't want to believe me, then there's nothing I can do about it."

Teresa and Heather stared at her, unconvinced. Danielle had to do something to distract them. . . . *That's it!* she thought, mentally snapping her finger. *Good ol' Lori to the rescue once again. Thanks, sweet coz of mine, for your weekend in the mountains.*

"I suppose you're not interested in a little piece of new gossip I just heard from Jane Haggerty. I was going to tell you about it, but if you're only interested in trying to convict me . . ."

"What gossip?" Teresa's ears instantly perked up.

"I don't know if I can trust you now," Danielle said teasingly.

"Come on, Dani, out with it," Heather said.

Teresa was practically jumping out of her skin. "We'll keep it quiet. Really."

Sure you will, thought Danielle bitterly. *Just like you'll keep quiet about Don and me if you ever find out for sure . . .*

Danielle didn't feel too great about sharing the rumor about her cousin Lori. She knew that Lori would never do anything like that to her. Still, Danielle was desperate. Anyhow, she reasoned, Lori would understand—she always understood. And besides, it was only a matter of time before everybody knew about her and Frank O'Conner anyway.

"Well," Danielle began, "I suppose it couldn't do any harm. But just remember, this story is top secret."

When Danielle had finished telling all she knew about Lori and Frank, Teresa gasped. "Wow! Hey, Dani, I guess Nick Hobart will be available pretty soon. Are you going after him again, or do *I* get a crack at him this time?"

Danielle didn't answer. She wasn't even listening. Out the window at Facades, behind Heather's and Teresa's backs, she saw Don James standing and dangling her car keys in his hand.

Danielle tried to keep her cool. She couldn't let them see him. *Come on, brain, don't desert me now*. Frantically, her eyes roamed all over the store and stopped at the unopened can of Diet Coke in Teresa's hand. "Can I have a sip of your soda?" she asked. "I'm dying of thirst."

"Sure," said Teresa.

Surreptitiously Danielle took the can from her upside down—she turned it over with a quick shake of her wrist. *There! That should do it*, she thought. All this time she kept them occupied with the last juicy details of Lori's weekend. "Only one bedroom in the entire cabin."

When Heather and Teresa looked at each other, Danielle flipped back the pop top on the soda can and showered her friends with a waterfall of Coke!

"Oooohhh!" Heather shrieked. "That stuff is all over me! I'm going to be a sticky mess!"

Danielle did all she could to suppress her laughter and act contrite. Finally, she'd given them what they so richly deserved! But she'd better cover quickly. "Oh, I'm so sorry. I had no idea you'd shaken it up."

"My suede pants!" Teresa screamed. "You've *ruined* them!"

"I really am sorry," Danielle said as sincerely as possible. "I honestly had no idea."

Teresa and Heather rushed to the ladies' room at the back of Facades to assess the damage. They'd be gone a good half–hour! *Whew.* The minute they were out of the way, Don popped in to see Danielle. *Saved*, she thought. *At least for now. . . .*

"Good news, Red," Don announced. "There's nothing wrong with your car."

Looking up from his perfect white teeth to his slightly crooked nose and into his deep dark eyes, Danielle felt her head swim with reckless abandon.

She walked up to him, placed her arms around his neck, and planted a sizzling kiss right on his lips. "There!" she said, reeling slightly from the heady rush. "That's to make up for the one you didn't get Saturday night."

What's happening to me, she thought, unable to take her eyes from his. She continued to hold on to his shoulders. *Could it be I'm falling in love?*

CHAPTER NINE

Lori had been in O'Burgers for about twenty minutes by the time Nick showed up. Not that she minded really—it gave her twenty minutes to go over her schedule for the rest of the week. Writing the lab report for biology on Sunday had taken time away from her other work, and she had to play catch-up.

After she finished working out her schedule, she ordered a club soda. *Where is he*, she wondered. *I hope nothing's happened. It just isn't like Nick to be late for a date.*

Just as she was about ready to go look for him, he appeared in the doorway. He looked tired as he waved and made his way through the crowded tables to the back booth, where he and Lori usually sat.

"Hi," said Lori. "What happened?"

"Nothing, really," mumbled Nick. "The store got real crowded right when I was about to leave. Some kids came in to buy equipment for the Atwood drama club, so I had to wait on them. You know, school loyalty and all that. We gave them a fifteen percent discount."

"Oh," said Lori, "anybody I know?" Merivale High kids and Atwood kids didn't usually spend much time together, but Lori knew a lot of them through Nick.

"Teresa Woods, Heather Barron, a girl named Jane Haggerty—that crowd."

"Oh." Those girls were the biggest snobs and gossips at Atwood Academy. Maybe they went to see if Nick had heard about Lori and Frank. "I didn't know they were into drama."

"Me neither. But they bought a VCR and a remote camera."

"Oh . . ."

Nick tried to smile at her, but it didn't work. "Nick?" Lori asked. "Is anything the matter? Did those girls upset you?"

It was the gossip, she could tell by his reactions. He could deny it all he wanted, but that was it. She was positive.

"No, nothing's the matter—not really." Nick *was* uncomfortable, and he kept swishing the ice in his water glass around and around and staring past her.

"Oh." Lori tried to relax and believe him.

Just then the waiter came up to take their orders. Nick and Lori both had the menu memorized and didn't have to refer to it.

When they were alone again, Lori looked over at Nick and smiled, but the smile just made her face feel unnatural and slightly contorted. He returned the same goofy look, and then they sat in silence as if they were strangers.

This is not fun, thought Lori.

The pressure of the unsaid was getting heavier by the minute. Finally Lori couldn't take it another second. "Nick, did Teresa and Heather say anything about—you know—what happened between me and Frank?"

Bull's-eye. She could tell from his face. "Oh, well, not much," he murmured. "Just some stupid stuff—you know."

"No, I don't know. Stupid stuff like what?"

Nick considered his answer a moment before he blurted it out. "Well, Lori, you didn't tell me you set it up to spend the whole day there. You said you went up just to get a field sample. I didn't know you drove up there intending to spend the whole day."

"Well, of course we had to—" Lori jumped to her own defense. "He said that we could get some real exotic stuff if we went to this pond in the woods near Oakdale. And Oakdale's a long way from Merivale."

"Well, what's wrong with the duck pond right here in Merivale? Or the nature preserve? They both have plenty of algae in them."

He was right, of course. Still, Lori tried to explain her reasoning at the time. "I thought it was a chance to get a solid A. I need an A in biology this year for my average so I can get a scholarship to college."

"Lori—" But Nick stopped himself from saying anything more. He put down his glass for a second and murmured, "Come on. Let's just forget it."

Just then the waiter arrived with their cheeseburgers and onion rings. "Listen," said Lori before she picked up her burger. "I made a dumb mistake going with him—I admit that."

Instead of that soothing Nick, it made him angry. "And I didn't know that whole thing about your clothes being wet. You wore his clothes up there? If you were wearing *his* clothes, what did *he* wear?" Nick said, forcing himself to keep his voice down.

"Frank wore his own clothes," Lori declared. "I had to wear his father's."

Nick raised one eyebrow now and shot Lori the kind of look she didn't expect from him. "And what was with the fireside dinner? That sounded pretty—romantic."

"Well, we had to eat, didn't we? And there was no heat, so we built a fire!"

Nick was not being Nick! He was being this other, jealous person, and Lori didn't like it one bit. She had to break the spell. She had to get through to him and reassure him. Didn't he know she would never do anything to hurt their relationship?

"Nick, look," she said, leaning in and whispering so no one could hear them. "This is ridiculous. Are you saying you think something fishy went on up there? Because if you are, why don't you just come right out and say it?"

She hadn't meant to say it that way. She sounded defensive and weird when she'd meant to be warm and understanding.

"Calm down, Lor—I don't *know* what went on up there. That's *all* I'm saying."

Lori looked down at her uneaten burger. If she had heard right, her boyfriend had just told her he was doubting her version of what happened over the weekend. That hurt.

"You say you don't know, but I told you everything earlier today!"

"A cabin in the woods, no electricity, a fireside dinner. It sounds pretty romantic if you ask me!" Nick's face was bright red and he kept clenching and unclenching his jaw. He looked ready to explode right there in

O'Burgers. Lori could hardly believe this was Nick.

"Well, it wasn't romantic—and if you still don't believe me—we might as well *break up!*" she said in a loud stage whisper that turned a couple of heads toward them.

The minute the words were out of her mouth, Lori felt like jumping across the table, throwing her arms around Nick, and telling him she loved him. How had all this other stuff happened?

Nick leaned back in his seat, his hand folded on the table, his knuckles bloodless.

"You want to break up, Lori?" His next words were slow to come, and when they did, he bit them off one at a time. "Well, that's just fine with me."

What? He hadn't really said that, had he? *No, Nick—you can't mean it!*

"Great!" Part of her watched herself in dismay as she stood up and picked up her coat. "Let's just consider ourselves broken up then! I don't want a boyfriend who doesn't trust me," she said, barely holding back the tears that were clouding her vision.

"I *do* trust you, Lori, it's not that. It's just that, well, I feel like a laughingstock, listening to everyone talk about you like that."

Lori wiped a stray tear from her eye. "Nick, how do you think *I* feel? It's me they're talking about, after all."

"Yeah, but you know the truth."

Lori couldn't believe it. "And *you don't?*" she asked, sliding back into the booth so everyone wouldn't overhear them.

Nick looked down at his plate. "I can't *know*, Lori. I can believe what you tell me, but it's not the same—it's almost like the truth doesn't matter anymore. Everyone already thinks the worst."

Hot tears were coming fast and furious now. Lori rubbed at her face with her napkin. "I thought you were going to stand by me," she said, her voice breaking. "But if that's the way you feel, Nick, our relationship really *is* over!"

Lori stood up and began making her way out of the restaurant. She kept her head down so no one could see the tears that were blurring the world around her.

"Oh, hi, Lori!" someone called out perkily from a table off to her left.

Lori looked and saw Gina Nichols seated with a few other girls from Merivale.

Lori didn't trust herself to speak, so she hurried out without stopping. How could Nick let her leave like this? And yet he was! Lori pushed through the door of O'Burgers and ran off down the promenade as fast as her legs would carry her.

CHAPTER TEN

"Hey, Red!" Danielle was on the ground level on her way up to the Body Shoppe for her twice-weekly workout, when Don's voice brought her to an abrupt halt. Seeing him trot down the promenade toward her, she instinctively looked over her shoulder to make sure none of her friends were around.

They weren't, but Danielle was not about to take any chances. Just because she'd kissed Don in Facades on Monday didn't mean she wanted the whole world to know about it on Tuesday.

As Don reached her, she took him by the arm and walked him off the promenade, through a metal door, and onto one of the mall's seldom-used service staircases.

"Ah, so you want to get me all alone,

huh? Why the hush-hush, Red?" Don smirked, pushing his glossy hair off his brow. "It's a little late to be keeping things between us under wraps. As far as I can tell, your prep school pals already know everything there is to know."

Danielle's face went beet red. Heather and Teresa couldn't be one hundred percent sure it was really her they'd seen in the parking lot that night. She'd gone to so much trouble to keep them in doubt!

"I don't know what you're talking about, Don," she said, trying to maintain her cool. It would be more than a little embarrassing if Don figured out how desperately she was trying to hide the fact that they had gone out. And she really liked Don and didn't want to hurt him. "What do you mean, they know everything?"

Don's dark brown eyes told her that he understood everything. He hadn't *told* her friends about their date, had he? If he had, she'd just have to leave town or go to boarding school.

"Well, I was just down in the arcade, and Teresa and Heather showed up—" he began, searching her eyes for whatever she might be feeling. "They pretended to want a lesson on Star Pirates, but I think they wanted to know who I was out with Saturday night."

Danielle's heart leaped into her throat.

"And what did you tell them?" she whispered hoarsely.

Don stood staring down at her with a crooked grin on his gorgeous face. "You're a funny person, you know it, Red?" he said, and reached out and gently placed his hand on her shoulder. "I know you're wild about me—you can't hide *that* from me—but you wouldn't be caught dead with me in public. And don't bother to deny it, 'cause I know it's true."

Danielle shifted her workout bag from one shoulder to the other and stared hard at the painted concrete stairs. What could she say? Don understood her. She could drop all her pretenses. She lifted her emerald eyes and looked at him openly, vulnerably.

"Oh, Don, you didn't tell them, did you?" she asked, barely audible.

Now Don looked away and shook his head. "No, Red, I didn't say a word. I just told them the truth—that who I was out with on Saturday was none of their business."

Danielle wished more than anything that she had the nerve to tell everyone how much she liked him—how funny and kind and gentle and mature he was. But she couldn't, and knowing that about herself made her feel sad and utterly empty. All she could do was murmur her thanks.

"Don, I know this must all sound so tacky. I mean—"

"You hit the nail on the head that time, Red. Frankly, I'm a little disappointed. I thought you were better than this."

"I thought I was too. I'm sorry. Please, please—don't be hurt."

Don leaned one arm against the wall and broke out in a lazy grin. "Don't worry about *me*, Red. I'm *proud* of who *I* am. Worry about yourself."

And before she had time to say another word, he was out the door and gone.

Tuesday morning Lori woke up with an incredible headache. All night long she'd had one nightmare after another. And the worst part was they were all about Nick.

In one of them, he and Frank O'Conner were whispering about her and laughing. In another, Nick was kissing another girl, some football groupie whose face Lori couldn't make out. In yet another, she was kissing Nick—except when the kiss was over, it wasn't Nick at all, it was Frank, and his hair wasn't hair, it was a disgusting smelly algae.

No wonder I've got a headache, thought Lori as she made her way to the bathroom and swallowed two aspirin. *There. Now all I've got to do is get through the rest of the day—and the rest of my life after that.*

Looking in the mirror, she saw that the whites of her normally crystal-clear blue eyes were red and puffy. She must have done a lot of crying in her sleep. Well, she had a right to cry—it wasn't every day a girl lost the most wonderful guy in the world.

And as if losing Nick weren't bad enough, she was going to have to go to school that day and pretend that everything was all right.

It isn't fair, she kept thinking. Her whole life was falling apart, and all because of some silly rumors.

When she got to school, Lori found Ann Larson waiting for her at the door. At least she could tell her best friend about the break-up. Knowing that Ann and Patsy would support her and help her through her bad time was about the only good thing in Lori's life right then.

"Lori, I've got to talk to you," Ann began, her gray eyes searching Lori's face, taking in the signs of Lori's overnight tears.

"All right. Tell me. What is it?"

Ann led Lori over to one side of the hall. "There are new rumors going around about you. I think you should hear them from a friend before you hear them from somebody else."

What more rumors could there be, Lori wondered, turning her face away. "Okay—fire away. What's the latest installment in the Lori Randall-Frank O'Conner fiction?"

"It isn't about you and Frank, Lor—" Ann said tentatively. "It's about you and Nick. They say you've broken up."

Lori wheeled around to face her friend. "What? But—how could anyone possibly know that?"

Ann's face grew concerned. "You mean it's *true?*" she asked.

Lori stifled a sob. "Yes, it's true," she whispered. "But how did it get around so fast?"

"Somebody apparently heard you arguing last night."

Lori's hand flew to her cheek in embarrassment. "You mean—? Well, we did have a pretty big fight in O'Burgers," she lamented.

"About what? You guys never fight."

"It was about Frank," Lori confessed. "Nick couldn't take all the rumors about us anymore. So I—well, we broke up, that's all—" Lori's eyes were brimming over with tears.

"Here," said Ann, offering her a handkerchief. "You'll need this. I think it's important for you to hold your head up high, Lor. You can't let all this awful gossip beat you, understand? I won't let you give in to it, and neither will Patsy. It's all too dumb for words. And Nick's going to realize that after he calms down."

Lori sniffed back her tears. "Oh, Ann," she moaned, "you're the greatest, did I ever tell you that?"

"Never mind me," said Ann quickly. "We've got to stop this rumor-mill churning—and fast. You and Nick will never get back together as long as people are still talking about you."

"Oh, he doesn't want to see me again," Lori said in despair. "It's over, and I might as well face it."

"Don't give up so easily, Lori," Ann cautioned her. "If it was me they were talking about, would you let me lie down and take it?"

"No." Lori gave a little laugh through her tears.

"Well, then—let's find the source, okay? Who could have started this latest rumor? Was anyone at O'Burgers during your fight?"

It only took Lori a split second to put two and two together. "Gina!" she cried. "Gina Nichols, that rat—it had to be her!"

It made perfect sense. Ever since the Atwood-Merivale football game, Gina had never gotten off Lori's case for one second. It would be just like her to spread the news that Lori and Nick were on the rocks.

"You can take care of Gina," Ann assured her.

But just then a horrible thought occurred

to Lori. "Ann," she said, "now that Nick and I have broken up, everyone will *definitely* believe that the stories about Frank and me are true. If it appears that Nick doesn't believe me, no one else will either. I'll never convince anyone of the truth. And worst of all, I'll have lost Nick forever!"

"Quit saying that, Lori!" Ann insisted. "You may have lost the battle, but the war's not over."

"Well, what do you think I should do?" Lori asked.

"For starters, have a little talk with Gina?"

Lori thought for a moment. "You know," she said slowly, setting her chin determinedly, "I think I will."

It was only eight-fifteen. Lori still had some time before homeroom. Trembling with emotion, she walked down the hall and found Gina's locker. Then she parked herself in front of it.

It wasn't two minutes before Merivale's head cheerleader showed up, her perky, strawberry-blond ponytail bouncing. "Oh, hi, Lori. How are you today? Love that blouse."

What a phony, thought Lori. "Gina—" she began, starting right at the heart of the matter, "I really don't appreciate your talking about me and Nick to other people. I want you to stop."

There. She had said it, and said it right out. A couple of Gina's friends joined them then.

"But, Lori," Gina said, "what do you mean? I never said a word about you and Nick, did I?" she asked another cheerleader who had walked up.

It was a bold-faced lie, and both Lori and Gina knew it. "Listen, Gina, my life is none of your business." The small group of girls, mostly Gina's friends, who had gathered around them now were eagerly drinking in every word.

"I'm sorry, Lori. I didn't know your breakup with Nick was a secret," Gina cooed.

"Lori broke up with Nick Hobart!" Lori heard one of the girls whisper to another.

What a nightmare! Maybe if she really appealed to Gina, really leveled with her— "Gina," she said, taking her aside, "don't you understand? If there's a whole lot of talk about me and Nick breaking up, people are going to think it's all true about Frank!"

"Well, gosh, Lori," said Gina with a snide smile. "Don't you think people have a right to believe what they want?"

Ugh. Lori wasn't getting anywhere, and the more she tried to talk to Gina like a human being, the worse it was getting. She'd have better luck talking with Frank.

"Never mind, Gina," Lori said finally,

making her way through the pack of Gina's friends. "Sorry I mentioned a thing!"

When the bell rang for third period classes, Lori went to her locker, gathered up her swamp water and lab report, and headed for biology class.

There was Frank, talking to one of their classmates just outside the classroom.

"Frank, excuse me, could I talk to you for a minute," asked Lori, trying to maintain a friendly tone.

"Sure, Lor," said Frank, giving her what he thought was a sexy leer.

"In private, please—"

"Whoa—all right, Lor!" Frank shot a look at the boy he was talking to, a look that said *Now do you believe those rumors?*

They walked to the end of the hall, where no one would be able to overhear what they were saying.

"Okay, Frank," Lori said evenly when she was sure they were alone. "This has got to stop. I mean really stop."

"What, Lori? What are you talking about?"

"Nick and I have broken up, Frank, and it's all because—"

"You and Nick? Broken up? Oh, that's really sad. Well, if you need a date for next weekend, I'm here, you know." Frank flashed her one of his roguish grins. "You know, you look great today."

"Oh, cut the garbage, Frank," snapped Lori. "This is serious."

"Okay," he said, suppressing a smile. "So, let's start again, okay. You and Nick broke up. That's really a drag. But you know something, Lori—you're too good for a guy like Nick anyway. What's he got besides brains and looks?"

Nick Hobart had a lot more than those things, but Lori wasn't about to go into it with Frank O'Conner. "I want the rumors about you and me in that cabin to stop, Frank," she said, her voice a shade lower than usual. "I really mean it. I want them to stop today!"

"But, Lori, I already told you, no one will believe a word I say! The more I deny the rumor, the more the guys believe it." With that, Frank shrugged. "Maybe we should just stop fighting fate and start going out." Now he was giving her a sickly smile, and Lori felt like punching him right in the nose.

"Thanks a lot, Frank," hissed Lori, her fury growing by the minute. "You're a real pal."

"Don't blame me if people are assuming the worst, Lori," said Frank, trying awfully hard to look innocent. "I'm not responsible for human nature, you know."

There was no sense talking to this jerk anymore, thought Lori. "Okay, Frank," she muttered, storming away.

As she walked into class and took her seat, the eyes of everyone in class were on her. Lori took two deep breaths, struggling for control. She had no idea how she was going to get through the day. No idea at all.

CHAPTER ELEVEN

Lori poured a mug of hot cocoa for herself and slumped over the old Formica counter in her kitchen, every nerve in her body defused. If it all wasn't so terrible, it would have been funny. Two hours earlier she was so angry she wanted to throw things, and now she hardly had enough energy to stir her drink.

Usually, when things got this bad for her, she'd call Nick. It was just so great to hear his voice. Nick was so understanding, so together—or, at least, that's what she had thought until the night before. But now calling him was out of the question.

Lori didn't even hear her mother come into the room. She was too busy thinking about how she'd never, ever, in a million years, get over Nick. It was the worst loss in her entire life, and she was sure that even when she got to be a little old lady, she'd still be hurting. Nick was just too good to lose.

"Hi, Lori. Lori? Hello." Cynthia Randall was standing in the door to the kitchen with two brown paper bags of groceries. She still had her nursing shoes and uniform on.

"Oh, hi," Lori said, popping up to help her mother.

"Why the long face?" her mother asked in a gentle tone.

Lori sighed. No sense getting her mother involved in all this. "Oh, it's nothing, Mom," she said in a super-quiet voice.

"You're upset about something, I can see that. Now, why don't you just tell me what it's all about."

"Oh, a lot of stuff," murmured Lori. "All of it stupid, and—oh—"

"Do you want to talk about it, Lori?"

"I don't think it would do much good. But thanks, Mom." She knew her mother cared, but after her Sunday morning confrontation with both her parents, Lori was still feeling a little raw.

"You never can tell," coaxed Mrs. Randall. "I can put this stuff away later," she said, pointing at the groceries. Then, she took off her coat and sat on a stool next to Lori at the counter.

"Come on, out with it," There was a sympathetic look in Cynthia Randall's eyes that Lori couldn't resist.

"It's such a mess, Mom. I don't even know how to begin. I guess it all started last weekend," said Lori shakily. "Word got out at school that Frank and I had been stranded at the cabin for the night, and now—well, everyone assumes something went on between Frank and me. And it didn't! It really didn't."

"I believe you, Lori," said her mother simply.

"Thank goodness you trust me!" Lori exclaimed. "You and Ann and Patsy are the only ones in the whole world."

"Oh? What about Nick?" Her mother's face had clouded up, and Lori knew she already suspected the worst. "Did you two have a fight over this?"

Lori couldn't help herself anymore. Her voice cracked and she said, "We broke up last night. At first he said he trusted me, but then he thought everyone was laughing at *him*. And that meant more to him than anything!"

Once Lori started sharing what was happening, she didn't want to stop.

"You know the dumb thing, Mom? Everyone's against me, and I haven't done a single thing wrong. I feel like I have to go around defending myself all day long, and still people don't believe me. Even my own boyfriend! *Ex*-boyfriend, I should say!" With a moan, Lori slumped over onto the counter.

Mrs. Randall gazed at her daughter thoughtfully. "Lori, can I give you a little free advice?"

"I guess so."

"Stop defending yourself. When people defend themselves, other people just assume something's wrong. But if you project confidence instead, and ignore the silly lies being spread about you, eventually you'll win everyone over. And if some of them don't come around? Forget them. Your true friends will be there for you, Lori. Even Nick." Her mother seemed so calm, so sure of what she was saying.

"You really think so?" Maybe her mother was right. Nothing else was working—she might as well give it a shot. Maybe she *had* been trying too hard.

"It's how you act that matters, Lori, not what you say."

"But, Mom, how could I possibly not act hurt? Or angry? I'm both of those things."

"It's hard, Lori. But it's worth it. Just tell yourself you're acting on the real truth, deep down inside. You have good values, and you're a good person. That's what counts."

"Thanks, Mom." Feeling a little better, Lori started putting the groceries away while her mother went to change.

From now on, Lori vowed, no matter how painful it felt, she was going to stop denying the rumors: Whoever believed her, believed her, and whoever didn't, didn't.

If only *Nick* would believe her . . . Was she really going to lose him? Was it possible their relationship could be over forever?

After the groceries were put away, Lori kissed her mom good-by, got her coat, and took off in her Spitfire for work. Going to work—in fact, going out anyplace to see people—was the last thing she wanted to do that night. Holing up in her room with the covers over her ears sounded like heaven.

But then, thought Lori as she made her way toward the mall, maybe being at work would be good for her. She could try out her mom's plan of action.

Lori turned the radio on, but when WMER played "Losing You Forever," she had to turn it right off. Getting through the night without crying was going to be a big enough challenge without certain love songs to set her off.

Just rise above the gossip. Her mother's ideas came back to her as she parked and made her way into the mall.

Lori held her head high as she pushed the door to Tio's open. "Hi, everyone!" she called out. That was the way she usually greeted her fellow workers, and that's the way she was determined to do it that night.

"Hi, Lori," said Ernie from behind the counter. *At least Ernie doesn't know about any of this*, Lori reminded herself.

"Coming through!" From the kitchen, Isabel Vasquez appeared with a tray filled with piping hot enchiladas. Her long black ponytail swung back and forth as she placed the tray down behind the service station. Lori walked over to greet her.

"I made these with a new ingredient, Lori. I hope they're not too spicy," said Isabel. "Ernie said to push the jalapeño peppers. See what kind of reactions you get."

"Okay," Lori responded. "They smell good."

"You must be hungry," said Isabel, wrinkling her nose. "Oh, Lori, I'm awfully sorry about you and Nick," she added sincerely. "I thought you two would stay together forever. You seemed so good for each other."

"I guess nothing is forever, Isabel." It was the only thing she could think to say. Throwing all the gory details at Isabel didn't seem appropriate to work.

"Ahem—"

Lori looked up and saw Jack Baxter standing on the other side of the counter. Jack was Gina Nichols's boyfriend, and the quarterback for the Merivale Vikings, and Lori had never really had a whole conversation with him.

"Are you available?" he asked with a funny smile. "I mean, for food."

"Sure am. These enchiladas are straight out of the kitchen. Supposed to be wonderful," Lori told him.

"I'll try a couple," said Jack, leaning on the bright orange counter. "So, Lori, what time do you get off?"

Lori stopped in her tracks for a minute. What did Jack Baxter care what time she got off? "Around eleven," she answered.

"Want a lift?" he offered.

That's odd. Lori got his order ready. "No, thanks. I have a car."

"We could go for a little ride, you know. And then I could bring you back here—" His voice was husky.

Lori faced him directly. If Jack Baxter was trying to ask her out, he was doing a pretty poor job of it. "No, thanks."

"I heard about you and Nick and all—"

Uh-oh, thought Lori. *Here it comes.*

"And I thought you'd like a little ride up to Overlook—I mean, I thought you'd be up for a good time now that you're, you know—available."

How dare he! Jack Baxter's snide implications were off base, off-color, and downright rude. In fact, he was acting like a creep.

Lori was just about to tell him exactly

what she thought, when she remembered the promise she'd made to herself.

"Sorry," she said as politely as she could manage, handing him his order. "You can pay at the cashier." With that, Lori spun around and faced the beverage server.

"Well, Lori—" she heard Jack say in the same snide manner. "If you change your mind, let me know."

Of all the nerve! Lori wanted to shout. But instead, she started rearranging the creamers as if she hadn't even heard him.

Instinctively, she gazed across the mall toward Hobart Electronics. She caught a glimpse of Nick. *Just my luck*, she thought, a lump rising in her throat as she watched him carry a heavy carton to the front counter. Was she dreaming, or did Nick look as sad as she felt?

Seeing him brought back all the good times they'd had together—all the parties, football games, and long drives—and all the times they'd stuck by each other. Could it really be over? Lori missed him so much.

"Hi," she heard a strange voice say.

She caught a tear with her finger before it ran down her cheek. When she looked up, a boy she didn't recognize was standing on the other side of the counter. He was kind of short and awkward. *Maybe from Atwood*, she decided.

"It's Lori, right?"

"Uh-huh," she mumbled. "What would you like? A taco? Enchilada? We've got a special on them tonight."

"Er, my name's Jeff—and what I'd like —um, well, if you're not busy Saturday night, I'd like—"

"Stop right there!" Lori snapped, slamming down her book of checks. "Listen, Jeff, or whatever your name is, I'm sure you're a very nice guy, but whoever told you I was available didn't know what he was talking about, okay?"

Jeff looked disappointed. "Oh," he said, reddening. "But they said you were—"

"I don't want to know what 'they' said, all right, Jeff? I plan on staying home Saturday nights—indefinitely. Now, if you don't mind, I have work to do."

Unfortunately, Jeff wasn't the last boy to ask Lori out that night. There must have been half a dozen in all, and, to make matters worse, the girls she knew from school completely snubbed her. Lori felt like a social outcast. Her plan didn't seem to be working very well at all. She knew that she had to stick to it, but she never expected it would be so hard.

Toward the end of her shift, she spotted Nick one more time. He wandered out of Hobart's and headed for the escalator. Now was the time he would usually come over to wait for her, and Lori couldn't help but wonder if he was on his way to meet someone else. Her heart sank. It was all so wrong. Why couldn't life be simple, like before? Why weren't she and Nick still together?

She walked to the door of Tio's and followed Nick with her eyes as he rode up the escalator.

Knowing the truth is one thing, she told herself, unable to hold back her tears another second. *Living with it is something else.*

CHAPTER TWELVE

At the Bootery, Danielle studied two pairs of shoes on the display rack, trying to choose between them. Somehow, shopping just wasn't doing the trick for her the way it normally did. Most of the time, when she had a problem, a little consuming took her mind off things. But now it was just the opposite.

Choosing. That was the problem, in life as in shopping. If she didn't choose soon between Don James and her friends, she would wind up with neither.

With a scowl, Danielle looked away from both pairs of shoes. Neither of them was perfect. Nothing was perfect anymore. It was getting Danielle super-depressed.

"Good evening, Ms. Sharp," her regular salesman said. "May I show you something?"

"Oh, not now, Charles." Danielle sighed. "I'm just not in the mood. Maybe tomorrow."

"Very well, then," said the disappointed Charles, holding the door for Danielle as she left and walked out onto the promenade.

As she headed toward the down escalator, she thought back to the little prank she had pulled with the soda can. She felt bad about it, but on the other hand, it had served her purpose well. She had managed to keep her date with Don under wraps, and best of all, Teresa and Heather had never looked so ridiculous. Still . . .

Passing by Tio's Tacos on the ground level, Danielle's thoughts turned to her cousin Lori. At least there was someone who was worse off than *she* was. It was slightly comforting, but only slightly. Besides, Danielle did feel bad about the little part she had played in spreading the story of Lori's weekend with Frank O'Conner.

And sure, Nick Hobart was available now, but Danielle didn't want him anymore, not really. All she could think about was Don James—the leathery smell and smoothness of his jacket, the way his hair fell over his forehead, that slow, almost mocking grin of his, and those eyes. . . .

Without even thinking, Danielle found herself wandering into a deserted Tio's Tacos. She didn't know why—she certainly

wasn't hungry, and if she was, she wouldn't
have gone to Tio's. Sure, the food was better
since Isabel Vasquez had taken over the cook-
ing, but the place still had no class. Teresa
and Heather wouldn't have been caught dead
there.

The minute Danielle caught sight of her
cousin's tear-stained face, however, some of
the thoughts of her problems went out of her
head.

"Lori!" she cried. "You look *terrible!*"

Lori, who was standing behind the counter,
sniffed back one stray tear. "Oh, hi, Dani. I
feel terrible. You know all about my little
problems—everybody in town does."

"Oh, Lori," said Danielle, taking her cousin's hand. "I feel so sorry for you."

And so guilty. Danielle bit her lip. She
felt ashamed that she had ever helped to
spread gossip about Lori. After all, Lori had
been her best friend in the world, and she'd
always been really good to Danielle.

"And I know none of the things they're
saying about you and Frank are true," she
added.

"Thanks, Dani," said Lori, wiping her
eyes with her forearm. "It means a whole lot
to me to hear you say that."

Danielle looked hard at her cousin. *That
could be me if the rumors about me and Don really
got started—and if Don dropped me*, she thought
soberly.

"What's the matter, Dani?" asked her cousin. "Here I am, totally absorbed in my own problems, and something's obviously bothering you too."

Danielle was taken aback. "Oh!" she cried, reaching into her purse for her compact. "Is it that obvious?"

"Well, no, actually," said Lori, hedging a bit. "It's just that, well, you usually don't come around here unless . . ."

"Unless I need something?"

"Oh, no! I didn't mean it that way."

"It's okay, Lor," said Danielle. Maybe because of her feelings for Don, she was more capable of understanding Lori now. "It's true. I guess I haven't been the best cousin to you—or a very good friend either."

"Hey, you've been just fine," Lori insisted.

"No, I haven't been," Danielle insisted. "Truth is, I *do* have something on my mind. Maybe you can give me some advice—since you're kind of in a similar situation."

"Really?" Lori sounded shocked. "But, Danielle, I haven't heard any rumors going around about you."

"Not *yet*, you haven't." Danielle sighed, sinking into a chair. "Do you have time to talk?"

Lori looked around at the deserted restaurant. Closing time was only fifteen minutes away. "Sure," she said, walking out from

behind the counter and leading Danielle to a
table. She took a seat across from her cousin.
"So what's it all about?"

"Oh, it's Don James. I had a sort of date
with him last weekend, and I didn't want
anybody to know about it. Only Heather and
Teresa spotted me with him. They aren't sure
it was me, but they're pretty suspicious, and
it's only a matter of time . . ."

Lori sat there listening intently, her blue
eyes wide and open. Danielle had forgotten
how great it was to have somebody like Lori
around, somebody who loved her just for
who she was.

"Anyhow, I guess I've got a choice to
make, huh?"

"Sounds like it," said Lori. "So what's it
going to be?"

"I don't know!" cried Danielle, grabbing
her hair with her hands. "Don is so, so different from me. He doesn't fit with the rest of
my life at all, and, of course, if I really started
dating him, all my friends would drop me
like a hot potato."

Lori gave a mirthless laugh. "Then they're
not very good friends, are they?"

Danielle bit her lip. The truth was hard
to take, but Lori was right. . . .

"Do you really like Don?" Lori asked.

"I think I do, Lor," Danielle answered.
"But, I mean, I don't know him all that well."

"Then, I guess, you'd better go out with him some more and find out about him. Believe me, Dani, when you find the right guy, don't give him up—not for *anything*. I know what I'm talking about."

Danielle looked at the open, honest look on Lori's face. "I'm going to tell them the truth, Lori. If Heather and Teresa don't understand, then they can take a hike."

She stood up, resolved to take action. "And thanks, Lori. I only wish I could help you as much as you've helped me."

Lori smiled. "I wish you could too," she said softly.

As Danielle started to slide into her car for the drive home, something shiny in the back seat caught her eye. It was the photos she and Don had taken on their date. *He must have put them back there!* she realized.

She picked up the pictures, and, looking at them, she suddenly felt warm all over. She remembered how much fun she had had with Don that night.

In one of the shots, he had his arm around her. She smiled, wishing she were in his arms at that very moment. He made her feel so *special*. Maybe that was what Danielle liked about him the most. She knew that Don would like her even if she were dirt-poor and didn't wear makeup or great clothes.

Suddenly she was struck with a pang of guilt. She wished she had the courage to admit to Teresa and Heather that she had gone out with Don James. Why hadn't she? Because Don just didn't fit in with the kids in their clique. If she had told Teresa and Heather, everything would have been out in the open now, and she wouldn't have had to worry about seeing him on the sly.

Would they understand, or would they turn it around and use it against me, she wondered. It was easy for Lori to tell her to trust Heather and Teresa with the truth, but could she? One thing was for sure—Danielle didn't want to end up like Lori, with everyone in town saying nasty things about her.

Danielle leaned against her BMW and sighed as she took one more look at the photos. *Mother would never approve,* she knew. *Neither would Dad.* It wasn't just Heather and Teresa and her friends Don didn't fit in with—it was her whole life!

Danielle hastily tossed the photos onto the back seat and climbed back in. She slammed the door shut, gunning the engine. Lori's words still rang in her ears. *When you find the right guy, don't give him up—not for anything. . . .*

But did she have the courage to tell her friends the truth? Did she?

CHAPTER THIRTEEN

As Danielle went to her locker to pick up her French book, she sighed. Ducking around Atwood, hiding from Teresa and Heather, was becoming exhausting. Maybe she should tell them.

Slipping a lipstick out of her purse, she coated her lips with some Perfectly Pink, and smiled into her locker mirror. *Oh, well,* she thought, at least she was still beautiful.

"Hi, Danielle." The masculine voice behind her was familiar. At one time, she would have flipped just to hear that voice calling her name, but not now. Now only Don could do that to her.

"Hi, Nick," answered Danielle, spinning around to face Lori's former boyfriend. "Are you walking to French?"

"Yeah," he said distractedly. "I'll wait for you. Hi," he said to one of his football buddies who was passing by.

"I'm sorry about what happened between you and Lori, Nick. I really am," said Danielle, meeting his aquamarine eyes with a sympathetic glance. She thought about how gossip and other people's opinions could really ruin a relationship.

"Thanks," he mumbled. "Nobody's sorrier than I am."

"But maybe the breakup doesn't have to be permanent. I still think you and Lori are a great couple. Maybe things will work out between you after all." She closed her locker door and started to join the traffic walking to classes.

Nick seemed very interested in what Danielle was saying, and held her back. "Have you talked to her?" he asked quietly so no one could overhear. "Did she say anything to you?"

Danielle sighed. "Oh, Nick, she's feeling awful about everything too! Maybe you two should get together and talk."

Just at that moment Teresa and Heather emerged from the crowd and stood opposite Nick and Danielle. The minute the girls caught a glimpse of them, they began elbowing each other and whispering.

"Look at that," cooed Teresa loud enough

so that Danielle, Nick, and anybody else nearby could hear. "I see Danielle isn't wasting any time."

Danielle's cheeks turned to fire.

Instinctively, Nick took her by the elbow and led her into the steady flow of students.

"Nick, I hope you don't think—" Danielle sputtered. There had been a time when she would have done anything to make a play for Nick. But that was all ancient history, and being reminded of it now was a just a huge embarrassment.

"Forget them," murmured Nick. "I'm so sick of people gossiping." He lightly punched his notebook.

"Hey, don't do that!" cautioned Danielle, giggling. "We don't want our star quarterback hurting his throwing hand."

Nick smiled. "You know, Danielle, you really are a nice girl. No wonder Lori always has good things to say about you."

Danielle blushed. "Oh, come now," she said modestly, lifting her silky red hair with her free hand.

"No, seriously," Nick insisted. "You're going to make some guy a fantastic girl friend."

It was really ironic, thought Danielle. At any other time she would have taken that opportunity to make a move for Nick. But now she just let it go by. Don was the only guy she wanted. And since their relationship was impossible, she'd just continue to play the field. As for Nick, he was Lori's guy, and that was that—even if he and Lori *had* broken up.

"So, you really think Lori would give me another chance?" he asked, his eyes lighting up hopefully. "I acted pretty stupid the last time I saw her."

"If you got down on your knees and groveled," Danielle joked. "No, seriously, Nick, why don't you try to talk to her. I have a feeling she'll listen." Danielle was feeling so guilty about spreading the rumors about Lori and Frank that she felt she had to get Nick and Lori back together.

"I'm going to do it," said Nick, suddenly smiling. "Thanks, Danielle."

"No, no," Danielle corrected him as they walked into French class. "That's *merci*, Danielle."

"Excellent work, Lori and Frank. An A plus!" Mr. Harris was beaming as he handed back the report Lori had written.

"You see, Lori? What did I tell you?" crowed Frank as Mr. Harris went on to the next lab table. "With my great idea, and your wonderful typing skills, we aced the project. We should work together all the time!"

"My *typing* skills?" Lori retorted. "Listen, Mr. Wonderful, you would have had an F without me. I did all the work on this little project. And let me tell you something else, Frank. There was a moment up there in the cabin when I thought you were actually an okay human being. 'He's just lonely,' I thought. 'That's why he always acts like such a jerk.' But I was wrong. Now I realize that you act like a jerk because you *are* a jerk—through and through. And frankly, I can't wait to flush these stupid jars of algae down the toilet and forget this whole rotten project!"

Lori didn't have to work until later that day. But she went to the mall right after school to shop, hoping she could take her mind off some of her problems.

Just a couple of weeks earlier her whole life had been beautiful. Now everything was a total mess. She wandered in and out of stores trying to interest herself in anything. She actually had a surplus in her savings account and could splurge if she wanted to. But nothing looked good. There was no getting around it. Life without Nick was just too awful.

She was walking by Aunti Pasta's, when she heard two voices coming from behind a five-foot plant that made her turn and stare down the concourse. She'd have known Nick's voice anywhere. And as for the guy he

was talking to, well, Lori had heard more of
Frank O'Conner than she ever wanted to.

"What are you saying?" Nick was chal-
lenging him. "That you're afraid to talk to
me? Is that it?" Lori had never, ever heard
Nick sound so angry before.

She ducked behind one of the huge round
pillars and sneaked a peek at the two guys.
Frank was looking down at his feet so he
wouldn't have to look Nick in the eye. Nick's
gaze never wavered from Frank's face.

"What's the big deal?" Frank was saying,
trying his best to sound casual, Lori thought.
"As far as I can tell, Hobart, you and I just
don't have anything to say to each other."

"That's where you're wrong," Nick said,
leading Frank to a bench so they could sit.
"We've got a lot to talk about!" Lori peered
around the pillar. Nick was practically breathing fire. "For starters, I'd like to know why
you went around spreading a lot of garbage
about the time you spent with Lori in the
mountains. Nothing happened between the
two of you, and I want to know why you let
people believe it did."

So, Nick did trust her! Lori's heart leapt.

"But I *didn't* say anything happened, Nick.
Honest I didn't!" Frank was stammering now.
"I can't help it if people jump to the wrong
conclusion about things."

"Oh, yes, you can." This was the old Nick, the one who trusted her. Lori glowed.

"I tried, Nick, honest I did." Poor Frank was attempting to sound so pathetic. Lori wondered if he thought Nick would beat him up.

"Do you realize the damage you've done?" Nick was leaning into Frank, forcing himself to keep his voice down. "Do you?"

Frank tried to smile, but it came out like a wince. "I really didn't mean to—I just thought—"

"No, you didn't. You didn't *think* at all, and worse, you didn't care! All you're concerned with is acting the part of the big man on campus. And that doesn't wash, O'Conner, because everybody knows you're a dork. Decent guys don't go around making up stories about girls—especially girls like Lori."

"If you want me to apologize, Nick—" Lori could hear the fear in Frank's voice even from a distance.

"What I want is for you to realize what you did! You hurt Lori! And she didn't deserve it. Not only that, you hurt a bunch of other people too—like me! All so you could have your fun and give your reputation a little boost. Well, you're in trouble this time, O'Conner, and you're going to pay for it." He stood up then and pulled Frank to his feet with one jerk at his shirtfront.

"What are you going to do? Punch me out?" Frank asked, practically nose to nose with Nick. "Go ahead, that'll cement things for good. After I show everyone my black-and-blue marks, they'll all think the rumors are true."

Lori continued to watch, quite openly now. Nick still had a fistful of Frank's shirt and he continued to stare at him, his right hand bunched into a fist. Slowly he tapped the fist against his leg. A small muscle in his cheek moved in and out. Other than that he was perfectly still as he decided Frank's fate. Finally, his hand unclenched and he let Frank go.

"You think you're pretty smart, don't you, O'Conner?" Nick fumed. "Well, maybe I won't have the pleasure of punching out your lights—but I want you to know that I wouldn't trade places with you for a million dollars. How you can live inside yourself is beyond me. You've got to be the creepiest person on earth, if not in the entire universe."

And with that, Nick stood up and walked off down the promenade, rolling his shoulders as he went. As Lori stood still, hypnotized by what she'd just seen and heard, Frank slunk off around the corner, looking for all the world as if he *had* been beaten up.

Lori knew right then that in spite of all that had happened, everything *was* going to be all right. It was just a matter of time. . . .

CHAPTER FOURTEEN

After having avoided Teresa and Heather all week, Danielle finally decided to confront them head-on. She was tired of avoiding them and playing games. She had been looking for her friends for fifteen minutes now. *Finally*, there they were, sitting at a front table in Cookie Connection, stuffing their faces with what looked like Death by Chocolate sundaes.

The front tables had a superb view of the ground-level promenade. Anything happening out there could be easily observed and stored up for the gossip mill. That was why Danielle and her friends spent time there. That, and the sundaes, of course.

"Hey, you guys!" cried Danielle, walking straight up to join them. "How've you been?"

Heather fluffed her raven hair and looked over at Teresa with lowered eyelids. What was Danielle up to? she seemed to be thinking. "Teresa," she said, "do you think we should forgive her for ruining our outfits?"

Teresa pouted, and put a finger on her cheek. "Hmmm—I guess so, *if* she's very, very nice to us from now on."

"Thanks, you guys!" cried Danielle, seating herself next to Heather. "Here, let me help you with your sundaes." Grabbing a spoon, she dug in before either of her friends could say a word.

"Give her an inch, she'll take your whole dessert," quipped Teresa, pulling her sundae out of Danielle's reach. "Hungry for love, Danielle?"

"Yeah," said Heather, "they say when you want a kiss but can't have one, you go for the sweets instead."

"Will you guys lay off?" Danielle said, rolling her eyes and putting down the spoon. "When are you going to let it rest?"

"When you come clean and admit you were out with Don James last Saturday night," said Teresa, leaning in and staring right into Danielle's eyes.

"What's the big deal, Danielle?" added Heather. "We don't care who you go out with. If you want to date one of the monkeys in the zoo, it's okay with us."

"Don James is *not* a monkey in the zoo!" Danielle blurted out.

Teresa and Heather looked at each other triumphantly. "Then what's he *really* like, Danielle," Teresa pressed her. "Tell us—is he a great kisser?"

"Are his arms strong and warm?"

"Does he whisper sweet nothings in your ear?"

Both the girls were giggling now. Danielle sat there, glued to her seat, forcing a smile while she was dying inside.

She'd come there to admit the truth to her two best friends, and there they were, making fun of her before she'd even opened her mouth!

"Let's say I *did* go out with Don James— and I'm not admitting I did, mind you—but *if* I did, so what? What's the big deal? You two act like he's completely bogus. But tell the truth—don't you think he's incredibly handsome!"

Teresa laid a manicured hand on Heather's wrist and murmured, "Oh, sure he's handsome, under all that grease and dirt."

Heather cracked up. "I wouldn't go out with him even if he were the most gorgeous guy in the world—he's so, so—"

"So *what*?" demanded Danielle hotly. "Why don't you just come out and say it, Heather? The real reason you wouldn't go out with Don James is that he's *poor*! He's *poor*, and that's what's wrong with him! Well, so what if he *is* poor? He's a whole lot better than some of the guys *you've* gone out with!"

The two girls were as silent as stones for a moment. Teresa fiddled with her spoon, and Heather tore at her napkin.

"Oh, all right," Danielle spat out. "I really don't see what all the fuss is about anyway. So what if I went out with Don James? Big deal. It was only one date. It's not like we're a regular item or anything."

"Then why did you lie about it in the first place?" Teresa looked absolutely insulted.

"Yeah! We're all supposed to be best friends. We're supposed to tell each other the truth!" Heather commented.

"Well," Danielle said hesitantly, "I didn't think you'd approve."

"I have to admit I am a little surprised, Danielle," Teresa stated bluntly. "Exactly why did you go out with him anyway?"

Danielle knew they'd never understand, but at least they were listening to her. And finally, they had stopped teasing her for one short moment.

"It's kind of hard to explain," she said. "Don is different from all the other boys I've ever dated."

"I won't argue with you there," Heather said a little smugly.

Danielle ignored her and went on. "It's not just that he's so good-looking—although I can't say I mind that. It's just—well, there's something special about him. He's fun and funny, and exciting, and kind. Besides, he's the only boy who's ever asked me out who doesn't care how rich I am, or where I go to school, or anything like that. He likes me for myself. Don makes me feel special—like I'm the only girl in the world."

Teresa's brown eyes widened. "Oooo, Heather, watch out—this girl's in love!"

Danielle smacked the table with her hand. "There!" she insisted. "That's just what I mean. How can you expect me to tell you the truth if you're just going to make fun of me?"

Teresa put her hands up in the air and nodded. "Okay, Danielle, I don't understand or approve. But I'll *try* to listen because we're friends."

Danielle went on. "I'm not in love with him, I'm just—in 'like' with him, I guess you could say."

"Oh, that's so *sweet*," Heather said a little too sincerely.

"Really. It's so noble of you to overlook Don's reputation," Teresa said dryly.

"He isn't bad," Danielle argued. "He's just a little—offbeat. And deep down he's so good." She was going to go on, but when she saw Teresa raise her eyes to the ceiling, she realized it would have been a waste of breath.

"Come on, Danielle, wake up. Everyone knows that Don James isn't a boy scout," Teresa pointed out. "Didn't it occur to you that going out with him might hurt your reputation?"

"Of course," Danielle shot back. "And that's why I wanted to keep our date a secret. And why I hope you won't tell anyone about it."

"Oh, well, don't worry, Danielle. We'll keep it quiet," Heather promised.

"Of course we will," Teresa said, nodding.

Danielle caught the two girls exchanging a furtive glance and wink. Danielle knew those winks, and she started to panic. *They'd better keep their mouths shut*, she said to herself. *Or I'll be social history if this gets out.*

The piercing sound of Jane Haggerty's voice suddenly interrupted her thoughts. "Slumming today, girls?" she asked, laughing. Jane, Atwood's own gossipmonger extraordinaire, was accompanied by Ashley Shepard. The two girls were practically inseparable lately.

"Have a seat," Teresa offered, gesturing toward the two empty chairs at their table.

"This isn't exactly L'Argent," Jane quipped. "But we'll just have to make the best of it."

She carefully brushed some cookie crumbs off her chair before she sat down.

"So, what's the latest?" asked Heather. Jane Haggerty could always be counted on for some juicy tidbits.

"Well, nothing's shaking at Atwood, but did you hear the latest about Nick Hobart? He and Lori Randall have finally broken up."

Teresa yawned. "That's old news, Jane," she remarked. "Tell us something we don't already know."

Jane glanced around behind her. "Patsy Donovan's not working now, is she? She's one of Lori's best friends, you know."

"In case you forgot," Danielle piped up, "I'm Lori's cousin. So just say what you have to say, okay?"

"Oh, but, Danielle, it's so hard to believe that you and Lori are actually related. You're so *different* from her!"

Danielle smiled, but she thought back to her conversation with Lori and decided that Lori and she weren't really so different after all.

"So? Don't keep us waiting. What's the dirt?" prodded Teresa.

"Lori apparently has been chasing Jack Baxter all over town. They've even made a couple of trips up to the Overlook," whispered Jane, sending all the girls into a fit of giggles. "Wait till Gina Nichols finds out."

"Sounds like fiction to me, Jane," said Danielle as lightly as she could manage. *Poor Lori! When are they ever going to stop trashing her?*

"Hey, you guys," Ashley Shepard broke in. "Aren't you going to the Atwood track meet? It's at four-thirty, you know—we don't have much time."

"I'll drive! Come on," Danielle volunteered, eager to change the locale and, she hoped, the conversation. She had had it with gossip.

Don would probably have laughed right in their silly faces, she couldn't help thinking as she led them out of the mall and into the parking lot.

"Your car looks fantastic, Danielle," Teresa said genuinely as they walked up to the white BMW with the SHARP 1 license plate.

"Thanks, I just had it detailed at this new—"

It was after she put the key in the lock and turned it that she saw them. The photos of her and Don were still in the back seat of her car! But it was too late. She'd already opened the car doors. Jane was climbing in the back!

"Let me clean up back there—it's a mess," said Danielle, climbing in and reaching over the front seat into the back of the car.

"Thought you just had the car detailed?" said Teresa with a quizzical look.

Danielle could feel them, her fingertips were just touching the end of the strip of photos, but they were still out of her reach.

"Hurry up, Danielle," said Ashley from behind her. "We're going to miss half the meet. What are you fumbling back there for anyway?"

"Oh, nothing," Danielle grunted, trying to make her fingers stretch just another half inch.

"Hey!" cried Jane as she slid in. "Do you mind? Your hand is right in my way! I'm going to sit on it."

Good! thought Danielle. *I just hope my hand's on the pictures.*

But it was too late. "Hey, wait a minute—what are *these*?" came Jane's insinuating nasal voice.

Danielle gasped and tried to grab the photos out of Jane's eager little hands.

"I don't believe it!" cried Jane triumphantly. "This just can't be! Look at these pictures, Ashley. Am I hallucinating, or *what*!"

"Give me those," Danielle demanded. She jumped out of the car and spun around to face Ashley, who had the pictures now.

"Danielle—and *Don James*!" gasped Ashley, her eyes wide as saucers. "Danielle, what on earth is going on?"

Danielle wanted to sink into the ground. Teresa and Heather might have been bribed to keep her date with Don a secret, but now that Ashley Shepard, and especially Jane Haggerty knew about it, it was only a matter of time before everyone at Atwood Academy— no, everyone in the entire town—knew everything that had happened between her and Don, and probably, a lot of stuff that *never* happened too!

She was sunk. Absolutely sunk.

CHAPTER FIFTEEN

Lori's shift at Tio's seemed to take forever that night. Every second, she kept expecting Nick to walk through the door. She had been so sure that he would come that night, but as evening ended, and still no Nick, she began to doubt.

Maybe he'd decided it was too late, that too much damage had already been done, that things could never be the same between them again. And really, she couldn't blame him if that was what he thought.

She was so lost in thought that she didn't see Don James approaching until he was right in front of her.

"Hi, Lori," he murmured shyly. "How are you?"

"Oh, hi, Don. Not so hot," she answered,

glad to see him. She had always liked him in spite of his reputation at school.

"Oh. That's too bad," he said, not moving. "Uh, listen, could I talk with you for a minute? It's about your cousin—"

Relieved that it wasn't about herself, Lori called out to her boss, "Ernie, can I take five?"

"Sure thing, Lori," came the reply. "But only five, okay?"

"Right." She led Don to one of the tables and took a seat opposite him. "So," she said, folding her hands on the table in front of her, "it's about Danielle?"

"Yeah." Don seemed a little embarrassed to be talking to Lori about personal stuff. She guessed he usually handled his problems on his own.

"It's like this," he began, looking down at her hands. He lifted his head, glanced at the door, and then finally his eyes rested on Lori's face. "I know Danielle likes me. I know it for sure. Just the other day, right upstairs in Facades, she kissed me. But now whenever she sees me she takes off—even when none of her fancy friends are around. I don't think I did anything, you know, it's just—I don't know what to think."

He sat there with his head down again, his stare boring right through the table. "I thought, since you're cousins and all—I mean, none of her friends would speak to me in a million years—so I thought I'd ask you for some advice, if you don't mind."

"No, Don, I don't mind, not at all." Lori smiled. "And if I were you, I wouldn't be so worried. It just so happens that Dani was in here the other day, and we talked—about you, to tell you the truth."

"You did?" Don looked up, surprised. "What did she say? If you don't mind my knowing, of course."

"No, I don't mind," Lori assured him. "She likes you, Don—a lot. She said so, and even if she hadn't said a word, I could tell by her face, you know? She really, really likes you."

"*But?*" asked Don, apparently hearing the "but" in Lori's tone of voice.

"Well, she's torn," Lori admitted. "You know that being accepted by the 'in crowd' at Atwood means just about everything to her."

"I know. I'd never embarrass her in front of them. But she cares about them too much, if you ask me," muttered Don angrily.

"I agree, but that doesn't change Dani, does it? I mean, Danielle is Danielle, and until she puts it all together—you know—" Lori gave Don a little smile.

"Anyway, my advice is, don't push her. I have a feeling she's going to tell them about you. And once she doesn't have to hide her feelings, well—"

"You think she'll go out with me again?" Don wanted to know.

"Well, I don't know the answer to that," Lori shrugged, "but if I were you, I'd hang in there and be patient. It may take her a while to come around, but sooner or later, I think she'll go for what *she* wants—not what her friends want. I hope so anyway, because I think you'd be really good for her."

Don smiled his crooked grin. "Thanks, Lori," he said softly. "You know something? Nick Hobart is one lucky guy."

Lori felt as if she'd suddenly been punched in the stomach. Apparently, Don James was one of the few people in town who hadn't heard about Nick and Lori's breakup.

"Nick and I—we broke up," she whispered sadly.

Don looked at her intently for a long moment. "Let *me* give *you* a piece of advice, Lori," he said, putting his forefinger under her chin and raising her face so she was looking at him. "Hang in there." And with a little pat on her cheek, he rose and strolled out of the restaurant, a confident bounce in his step.

Lori looked after him, smiling. *Yes*, she thought, *Don James really is a neat guy. And he would be good for Danielle. . . .*

After work at eight o'clock Lori wandered

down to the loading dock, the place where
her romance with Nick had first begun. It was
their place, an unlikely place, to be sure, but
just the same, it was full of happy memories
for her. Now, however, just standing there in
the semidarkness made her heart feel as if it
would burst.

"Lori?"

Lori gasped at the whispered sound so
close to her ear. Spinning around, she found
herself looking directly at Nick. His hands
hung uncomfortably at his sides, and he was
leaning forward, gazing into her eyes. Neither of them moved or said a word for what
seemed like minutes. "I knew I'd find you
down here," Nick said, breaking the silence
finally.

"I just got off work."

"I know. I went to Tio's."

She looked surprised. "You did?"

"I have to talk to you, Lori."

"All right."

"I want to apologize," he said gently. "I
shouldn't have let all that junk get to me."

Lori held her breath for a moment, tears
beginning to pool in her eyes. It was almost
too good to be true! "What about all that
'laughingstock of Merivale' stuff?" she asked,
sitting on a crate, not trusting her legs to
support her any longer.

Nick sat down beside her, but not touching her. "Look, Lori, I've been doing a lot of thinking lately, and—I feel like a complete jerk. I was very confused that night at O'Burgers."

"You could have fooled me. I thought you laid your feelings right on the line," she said, staring straight ahead.

Nick's aquamarine eyes were round and liquid as he gazed at the opposite wall also. "Please let me explain. The problem wasn't the gossip. It was the way it made me *feel*. I know this sounds selfish, but I was humiliated by the whole thing. That was *you* everyone was talking about, and there was nothing I could do to help. I never really doubted you for a minute, Lori. Honest. But all those rumors made me feel like a fool."

"How do you think *I* felt? I was the one taking all the heat."

"I know. I should have been more sympathetic. Maybe I should have tried to help, but I didn't know what to do." Nick suddenly turned and looked at her, grinning slyly.

Lori stiffened. "How can you smile at a time like this, Nick? What could possibly be funny?"

"I hate to admit it, but I think the main problem was that I was—well, jealous, in a way."

"Jealous?" Lori asked with amazement.

"Yeah. I mean after all, if you were going

to get a bad reputation, so to speak, you should have gotten it with *me*, not that O'Conner creep."

With that, they both burst out laughing.

"Nick Hobart, what am I going to do with you?"

"You could forgive me, for starters."

"Well, I don't know," she said teasingly. "I sort of understand what you're saying. If you must know, I've been feeling pretty bad the past few days too. I guess I was just as selfish as you were. I never stopped to think about *your* feelings. Can you forgive *me*?"

Before Lori could say another word, Nick put his arms around her and brushed her lips with a gentle kiss. She felt her pulse quicken.

"Does that answer your question?" Nick whispered.

"Perfectly," she answered with a warm smile. "But there's just one thing I don't understand."

"What's that?"

"Why didn't you explain this to me before?" she asked.

"I didn't realize it before," he admitted. "I was too mixed up!"

"Me too," Lori confessed. "I've been a wreck!"

"I was so furious at O'Conner that I never thought about anything else," Nick told her. "And then when I had the chance to knock him flat today, I couldn't do it. I realized it wouldn't make me feel any better, and I knew then that I had to get things straightened out with you."

Lori smiled. "I saw the whole thing," she whispered with a little giggle.

Nick's eyes widened. "You did?" he said. "What would you have done if I *had* socked him?"

"Oh, screamed probably," Lori replied. "I know you would have been punching him for *me*, and we all know Frank would deserve it. Still, violence never really solves anything."

"I know," said Nick, nodding his head.

Lori laughed, and ran the back of her hand over Nick's cheek. "You're too much, Nick Hobart, you know it?"

"We belong together, Lori," Nick said, taking her hand. "We really do."

"I know. I missed you, Nick."

"I missed you too. But just promise me one thing."

"What?" she asked.

"No more bio projects in the mountains, okay?"

She smiled coyly. "Deal."

"And if we ever get away for a vacation, it's definitely *not* going to be in the mountains! Maybe the beach . . ."

Laughing together and holding hands, the two of them headed back upstairs.

CHAPTER SIXTEEN

Lori knew she was at least a foot off the ground as she strolled down the promenade with Nick. She didn't know how she'd managed the past few days without him.

As for the gossip, well, there wasn't much she could do about that. She knew she still had to be the number-one item in Merivale. It wasn't fair, but it didn't matter all that much anymore. She had Nick back, and Patsy and Ann were behind her too. Her parents were on her side—what the rest of the world thought didn't mean too much.

Maybe when the kids saw that she and Nick were back together, they'd realize the rumors *couldn't* have been true. She knew it was going to be a very slow process. A lot of damage had to be undone.

"Remember this fountain?" Nick asked as they passed by the wishing pool.

"Are you kidding? How could I forget? It's where we first met."

Nick laughed. "Your copy of *The Old Man and the Sea* went flying into the water—appropriately!"

"Thank goodness you saved me from falling in after it!"

Nick reached into his pocket and pulled out a brand-new penny, which he tossed into the fountain. "Quick. Make a wish."

Lori closed her eyes. *What I want more than anything else in the world is for Nick and me to stay together forever.*

"What did you wish?" Nick asked.

"I don't think I should say," Lori hedged.

"Why not?"

"It's bad luck to tell," she murmured. "And this is one wish I *really* want to come true."

Nick smiled, squeezing Lori's hand gently. "Oh, that's just some old superstition."

"Okay, then, what did *you* wish?" she asked.

Nick tenderly stroked the wispy hair that framed her face. "I wished that your wish would come true."

Lori gazed into his blue-green eyes and smiled. "You really *are* the best, you know that?"

Just then, a whiny, nasal voice called out to them. "Nick! Lori! Yoo-hoo!"

Jane Haggerty came barreling toward them. "Are you two back together?" she asked. "Isn't that wonderful! Wait till I tell everyone. Oh, Nick, you're so forgiving!"

Lori and Nick smiled at each other. Jane Haggerty really was too much.

"Well, this is one big item to pass along," Jane crowed happily. "I suppose you've both heard the *really* hot news? After all, Lori, she *is* your cousin—"

Jane gave Lori a meaningful stare. "No?" she asked incredulously. "Well, get this—Danielle is going out with Don James! Is that a hoot, or what?"

Lori frowned. Was gossip going to hurt Danielle as it had her? Lori hoped not.

"Well, I'm off to spread the good word," said Jane happily. "Ta-ta. I'm *so* happy for you both!" And she was off in a flash.

"Well, Lor," said Nick. "It looks like your hour in the spotlight is over."

"Thank goodness." Lori sighed. "Now maybe I'll be able to walk down the hall in school without everyone snickering—but, oh, poor Danielle!"

"Mmmm—" said Nick, shaking his head and squeezing Lori's hand. "It is a shame. I'm finally beginning to realize that your cousin's really an okay person after all." Lori looked at him, surprised.

"We had a little talk," Nick explained to her.

Lori smiled. "The thing I feel worst about is *I* told her to tell the truth about it to her friends."

"You did?"

"Uh-huh. And now look at the mess I've gotten her into."

Nick enfolded her in his strong arms. "Don't worry, Randall. Everything will work out, you'll see. Danielle is someone who can take care of herself. And the same goes for Don James."

It was true, Lori had to admit. Danielle was a fighter, and never more so than when the odds were most against her. She'd be all right, Lori was sure of it.

"Besides," Nick added, "your advice was good. *Nothing* is better than the *truth*, and nobody knows it better than you and I."